rather be

a *Songbird* novel

MELISSA PEARL

www.melissapearlauthor.com

*****

*****

www.maeidesign.com

ISBN: 1545514879
ISBN-13: 978-1545514870

NOTE

For previous Songbird Novels, I have placed the playlist here, but one reader suggested to me that I should put it in the back, as the song list can give too much away. So that's what I've done. If you'd like to see it first, you are welcome to flick to the end of the book to check it out.

For Against the Current

I can't even explain what it is about this band, but I can listen to them constantly and not get sick of them. They are just my style and I've used a bunch of their songs in this book as a way to say 'Thanks for being awesome!'
#musicmakeseverythingbetter

ONE

NIXON

Snow.

Who knew it'd disrupt my life so badly.

I was an LA boy, used to blue skies and sunshine.

But there I was in JFK Airport, New York, hampered by piles of snow.

Did I seriously want to live there?

That was the big question, the one that brought bile surging up my throat whenever I thought about it. Mom said it was just nerves, and she was right. She told me I'd never been great with change.

"When you were a boy, we had to give you

warnings about everything. You were so nervous and jumpy. You always felt safest when you knew the plan." She laughed whenever she said those things to me, like the memories were sweet treasures to hold on to. Then her eyes would mist over and I knew she was thinking about my older sister, Reagan. She'd been nothing like timid little me. Impulsive was more her style—impulsive, bullheaded and insane.

I tried to shrug off the morose thoughts and focus on problem-solving my way back home, but the idea of how Reagan would handle the situation niggled at the back of my mind. She wouldn't have been irritated by the snow. Hell, she would have seen it as a challenge. Something else to conquer. Knowing her, she would have dragged our butts back to the city to live it up for the night—party until the flights resumed again. Or worse yet, she would have chatted up some random strangers and found us a ride home—one vehicle after another.

Squeezing my eyes shut, I pinched the bridge of my nose and played a round of dodge 'em with my brain.

My sister had only been sixteen when she died. I'd been thirteen at the time and it shattered me. It shattered everyone.

It was like the lights in our house went off all of a sudden, and no one knew how to switch them back on.

Mom spent the next year wavering between numb sadness, angry outbursts, and tearful despair. I didn't know how to handle it, so when she cried, I'd give her a hug. She'd hold me tight and whisper, "What would I do without you?"

Dad had never been good with tears, which made him quiet and grumpy. Since he couldn't control Mom's fluctuating emotions, he set out to control every other aspect of his life. He was desperate to fix things, to return some sense of normalcy to our home.

But how did we make things normal again when the loudest, most vibrant member of the family had been ripped out of our lives without warning?

When I wasn't trying to comfort Mom, I shut out the world, withdrawing from everyone at school so I didn't have to talk about my sister and her tragic end.

Thinking about her hurt. We hadn't been best buds or anything, but I still missed her. She was sunshine and laughter…just like another girl I knew.

The one who saved me.

My eyes shot open and I shook my head.

Don't frickin' go there, man.

The pain of losing her was worse than mourning Reagan.

I needed to get the hell home and back to the safety of my stable, uncomplicated life. The one where I knew what was coming and didn't have to worry about people disappearing or letting me down.

Sure, I was restless some days, but at least I knew where I stood. My life had been mapped out, charted carefully, and Columbia Law School was next on the agenda.

Everybody was happy about that.

I nodded, reminding myself that I was too.

It was a good plan.

But one random springtime blizzard was going to change all of that.

"Spring," I muttered, staring up at the flight board and cursing the word CANCELED. "It's not supposed to snow in spring."

Flustered travelers buzzed around me—pulling suitcases, calming partners and whining children, making unwanted phone calls.

Yanking out my phone, I hovered my thumb over the screen, already dreading the one call I had to make. She'd be pissed. It was out of my control, but she'd still be pissed. Well, not pissed…disappointed.

I was supposed to spend spring break with my girlfriend. Get some one-on-one couple time just hanging out together. I'd promised her. I'd specially caught the red-eye flights so I could be in New York City for the shortest amount of time possible.

If life was fair, I'd be checking in and hanging around for my 10pm flight back to Los Angeles.

I'd been in the Big Apple for less than twenty-four hours, and my body was hating me for it.

Sleeping on a plane was impossible.

I'd arrived blurry-eyed to meet up with a law professor buddy of my dad's. Having finished my online interviews, my parents thought it'd be a good idea to check out the school in person. So to save myself weeks of nagging from the ones I loved, I jumped at the first chance of getting a personal tour from one of Columbia Law School's most highly regarded professors. He was friendly and seemed impressed with my UCLA grades, but stayed pretty tight-lipped when I tried to find out if I had a shot at getting in to the prestigious East Coast college.

God help me if I don't.

My shoulders were aching under the weight of expectation. Between my girlfriend, Shayna, and my parents, they had me pretty well covered. I was the golden son and the perfect boyfriend. Because that's what they needed me to be.

So I kept pushing. Kept being what I was supposed to. Kept making them proud.

I grimaced. Pride would not be in the cards after I made this phone call.

With a reluctant sigh, I pulled up Shayna's number and pressed the green circle on my screen. I raised the phone to my ear and looked across the agitated crowd while I listened to the ring.

And my world stopped moving.

Like a mirage from the back recesses of my memory banks, she stood before me.

Charlie Watson.

My best friend from high school. The girl with the wacky sense of fashion and a personality so big it could barely fit into a room.

My eyes traveled down her body, quickly capturing the checkered skinny jeans, bright purple

Doc Marten boots, and the fitted Snoopy sweater. She had a big camera slung across her body, resting against her hip like it always did.

Man, she hadn't changed a bit.

The only difference was the blue dye at the ends of her long brown hair. It was a vibrant royal blue that made me grin. She always liked to make a statement.

Flicking the long strands over her shoulder, she stared at the flight board with a glum smile, then turned to her left and spotted me.

She froze. Her lips parted and her hazel eyes rounded in surprise. Then her chest jerked like she was choking on something, her face bunching with a powerful sadness. For a second, I thought she was going to burst into tears, but then she started blinking really fast and this shaky laugh popped out of her mouth.

I didn't know what to do, except hang up the phone and slip it into my pocket. The world around me dissolved as everything but Charlie became a blur.

She'd always had that effect on me.

The one person I could never let myself think about was suddenly the only thing I could see.

With a quivering smile, she hid her face behind her camera and snapped a photo of my stunned expression, then let out a low chuckle that reminded me of the girl I once knew.

She started closing the gap between us.

I wasn't sure how to feel at first. When she reached me, did I wrap my arms around her? Or did I push her away because she'd hurt me so bad?

Four years of radio silence.

I'd accepted the fact that I'd never see her again.

Yet there she was, weaving her way towards me.

One step closer.

Then another.

And she was near enough to touch.

I swallowed and let out this breathy kind of laugh, trapped in the surreal moment with no way out.

Was I dreaming?

"Hey, Nix," she whispered, her eyes glassy as she stepped forward and took me back to high school.

Her blue hair tickled my face as her slender arms wrapped around my neck and her black-painted fingernails clutched my sweater. Her trembling breath whistled against my ear, and in spite of all the unanswered questions, the deep bruising that I thought would never heal, I could do nothing else but wind my arms around her waist and hold on tight.

TWO

CHARLIE

It was Nixon.

And he was holding me.

Just like he had in high school.

Just like he had that summer.

I rested my chin on his shoulder and squeezed tight, never wanting to let go.

I couldn't believe it. After all those years of missing him, there he was.

His arms slackened around my waist and he pulled back, staring down at me. I studied his long, oval face. Still the same, yet different. His dark hair was even neater than it used to be—short at the sides and combed back, held in place with military-grade hair product. His mom must love it.

I resisted the urge to roll my eyes as I smoothed my hand down his sweater, then tweaked his collar.

"Wow," I murmured. "It's you."

"It's me." His soft whisper made me wonder if I'd been forgiven, but then I glanced into his brown eyes and had to concede that walking out on our friendship without a word probably had a lasting impact. One I wasn't quite ready to face.

So, in my usual style, I squeezed his arm and let out a laugh that was light and fresh. I couldn't ruin this precious moment with angst and heartache. I was standing beside Nixon. That was my happy place, and I had to make the most of it.

With a little grin, I nudged his elbow. "Of all the airports in all the world, huh? What are you doing in New York?"

His stunned surprise was making way for a smile. His lips twitched, nearly rising as he tried to answer me.

"I'm, uh…" The phone in his pocket cut him off.

Pulling it out with a fleeting wince, he checked the screen and I swear his shoulders slumped.

With a forced smile, he slid his thumb across the screen and moved away from me.

I studied him while he chatted to… Man, it had to be one of his parents. The way he was running a hand through the back of his hair, grimacing, pointing up at the flight boards. Stress pulsed out of him, and that look he used to get whenever he'd let his mother down flashed across his face.

Damn, I hated that.

Nixon was perfect, and the amount of pressure his parents always put on him drove me nuts.

I mean, yeah, upon reflection, I get that they wanted a good life for him. Nixon was their only son, made even more precious by the fact that they lost their firstborn in a reckless accident where safety had taken a back seat to thrill seeking. It happened when Nixon was thirteen. Against her parents' wishes, his older sister, Reagan, had taken off on a camping trip to Joshua Tree National Park with some seniors from school. Her boyfriend at the time had convinced her to try free-climbing with him. One slip and her life was over.

It hit the family pretty hard.

Nixon withdrew from everyone, turning his back on all the friends he once had.

He even ended up going to a totally different high school…which was lucky for me. I never would have met him otherwise.

I still remember the first time I saw him—the sad, quiet soul. The perfect A student. The golden son.

Since Reagan's death, he'd worked overtime to try to help his parents overcome the tragedy. He told me that he'd been stuck in a fog for a while but he clawed his way out of it, starting a new school, trying to get on with life and make the gaping hole just a little smaller. He'd tried to become everything his parents wanted him to be in order to dull the pain and make things better.

He was well-behaved, smart, talented and disciplined. Basically capable of becoming anything he wanted.

But that wasn't the point.

Because his parents weren't just going to let him become anything. He was their precious son, and they wanted him to have a sensible, secure life with a safe, predictable future—a stable job, a gated house, a handpicked wife and a bulletproof car.

I rolled my eyes as the sarcastic thoughts burned the back of my brain.

They'd go out of their way to minimize all risks in a bid for their son's longevity.

The deep sadness I had to constantly dodge rolled through me.

I was never quite sure what to do when it hit. Sometimes I got mad at them, and then myself, occasionally Nixon, or his reckless sister. Other times I cried. Most times I lifted my chin and reminded myself that I'd done the right thing.

It'd just be really great if when I did that, I actually believed it.

Nixon slid the phone back in his pocket and pressed his lips together. It was good to see his standard expressions hadn't changed since high school.

Heavy sighs, lips pressed tight, slumped shoulders. He was pissed off.

When he turned toward me, I made a funny face, hoping to break him out of his stupor.

His lips twitched and he closed his eyes, shaking his head as he shuffled back to my side.

"Damn this snow, right?" He glanced up at the boards again. "I can't see those canceled signs changing any time soon."

I followed his line of sight, then gave him a glum smile. "Probably not."

He clenched his jaw, and my stomach pitched. Damn, that was sexy. Call me weird, but I'd always had a thing for Nixon's jaw clenching. The way the muscles on his strong face tightened for a second. I wanted to touch his cheek, run my finger down to his chin.

Kiss his lips.

I squeezed my eyes shut and looked to the floor. He'd never been my boyfriend, and he probably never would be. Kissing was off the table, whether I wanted it to be or not.

But that didn't mean we couldn't hang out and have some fun. Yeah, mega-awkwardness was a possibility, but if I kept it light and fun, pretended that the last four years hadn't existed, hid my pain behind a bright smile, then maybe we could capture a moment in time. We could create a memory that would make us smile somewhere down the road.

Clearing my throat, I caught his eye and gave him my best grin. "So…the *rents* giving you a hard time, huh?"

He snickered, flashing his straight, white teeth at me. I used to say that to him all the time, and his reaction told me he hadn't forgotten.

I missed us.

Swallowing the lump in my throat, I kept my

grin in place while he answered me.

"Something like that. I'm supposed to be back in LA for spring break."

"Oh boy." I bulged my eyes, knowing just how much he was saying with those two short sentences.

World crisis! The plan's been changed!

I kept my sarcastic murmurings locked inside my mouth and overrode them by softly stating the obvious. "I bet they're pissed about those canceled flights."

"Disappointed." Nixon's head bobbed.

"Nothing you can do about them though, right?"

His thin lips turned into a fleeting pout as he shook his head.

So I did the only thing that was left to do.

Grabbing his hand, I gave it a jiggle and said, "Let's go have some fun."

"Uh…" The look on his face brought back a rush of memories that nearly made my eyes water.

"Come on, Charlie, don't do this to me again. Don't pull me out of my comfort zone."

I'd been torturing him ever since we started hanging out junior year.

But I'd never lost.

Because deep down, underneath all that ordered discipline and analytical thought, lay a guy who just wanted to break out and have a good time.

I wiggled my eyebrows at him. "Come on, you know you want to."

He turned his grimace into a strained smile. "I

don't know, Charlie. I should probably stick around, just in case..."

"In case what?" I laughed. "In case the weather suddenly clears? You know that's not happening. Let's at least go have a drink and catch up. You can come back and join the line later. I bet it will have barely moved by the time we get back."

He sighed at my logic, knowing I was right. "I shouldn't leave the airport though."

"That's cool." I shrugged. "You got a million bucks? I'm sure that'd buy us a drink or two at one of these airport bars."

He laughed and shook his head, then pressed his lips together and looked down the line.

The counter was at least twenty people away. He wasn't getting near that thing any time soon.

Letting go of his hand, I started doing a little dance and whistling a song from years ago—"Don't Worry, Be Happy." It used to irritate him, but for some reason it would always win him over in the end. He was a worrier, and there was nothing more triumphant than pulling him out of those frowny faces he made.

His eyebrows dipped in the middle, so I whistled a little louder.

"Stop," he whispered out the side of his mouth, looking around and giving the guy next to us an embarrassed smile. "Don't whistle." He cringed.

I grinned and started singing.

His eyebrows popped high. "And now you're singing. With the accent too. That's not embarrassing at all."

I laughed and kept going, tugging on his wrist and easily pulling him out of the line.

His eyes warmed with a familiar affection that I could feel all the way to the tips of my purple boots.

It was just like old times. Me pulling a reluctant Nixon away from his straight-laced, ordered life to show him a slice of something he never got at home—spontaneous fun.

THREE

NIXON

It was so familiar, Charlie dragging me into something I'd never do on my own.

If she hadn't shown up, I would have waited in that line all night.

As predicted, Shayna was pissed about the snow. She wasn't mad at *me,* per se, but it sure felt like it when she was complaining in my ear that I'd promised to be home so we could spend spring break doing…

I glanced down at Charlie's blue hair, the feel of her tiny fingers around my wrist.

Part of me wanted to shake myself free of her,

but a bigger part understood that I'd never be able to. She'd be with me for life, no matter what I did.

My swallow was thick and audible as we stopped outside a restaurant.

"They serve beer. We're all good." Charlie wove through the tables and lined up behind a couple of tired travelers.

I pulled my wallet out of my pocket while Charlie messed around with her bag, eventually yanking out a homemade-looking thing with bright orange, red and pink stripes and a long leather tassel attached to the zipper. I had to smile. I'd always loved her color. I grew up in a world of navy blues and gray. She grew up on a rainbow.

While we waited our turn, she looked up at me. "So, why are you in New York?"

"Oh, I, uh…I was visiting Columbia Law School. One of the professors gave me a tour, because…well, I've applied to go there."

Her smile was slow, but eventually spread across her face as she nodded. "Good for you."

She swallowed and looked away from me, making me feel like I'd somehow let her down.

The thought riled me but I didn't want to let it show, so I gently nudged her with my elbow. "How about you? What brought you to the Big Apple?"

She tapped her camera. "Just scouting some good locations. I'm doing freelance jobs, but the main company I work with does weddings, and one of their couples is determined to get hitched in New York, even though they're from LA. But they have visions of photos in Times Square and leaning against the golden bull. So, it'll be a weekend trip to New York in May."

"Why didn't they just get New York people to plan the wedding?"

"That's what I said, but Sarah and Justin, the wedding planners, are happy to do it. It's income for them, and they like to have as many face-to-face meetings with their clients as possible. So the fact that the couple lives in LA is convenient, I guess." She shrugged and brushed her hand through the air. "I don't know. It's actually pretty cool that this couple is doing something outside the box. I admire that. Plus it got me a free trip to New York, so I'm not complaining."

I snickered. "That is pretty cool."

"I'd hate to live here though. I mean, I love how alive and interesting the city is. So much color. But..." Her nose wrinkled. "Too much concrete."

My heart squeezed and my stomach bunched into a tight knot. I didn't want to think about the fact that if I did get into Columbia, *I'd* be moving to "the concrete jungle" in August. I wasn't ready to face that part of my life yet.

There was still a chance that I wouldn't get in.

Shayna would be gutted; she wanted to move to NYC more than anything. And my parents would be horrified. Their son never failed.

Which was why I gave the interview my best shot. It was the right thing to do. It made the people I loved happy, and that was important.

"So, why law school in New York?" Charlie

studied me, peeling back layers like no one else ever could.

I ran a hand over my hair and patted the back. "Oh, you know, I just want to try something new, and Columbia is a top school, so…"

"Your parents want you to go there, don't they?" Charlie's voice was dry and I'm pretty sure she rolled her eyes as she spun away from me to order our drinks.

I stuffed my wallet back in my pocket when she insisted on paying for both of us. I said I'd get the next round. She wasn't my girlfriend. Never really was. Never would be.

Besides, she wasn't the type to let some guy look after her that way. A free spirit was the best way to define her. Like a wisp floating on the breeze that you could never catch because she'd change direction on you last minute.

Unlike me—a solid rock, safe and unmoving.

I clamped my teeth against the biting pain that still stung even after all this time. It was tempting to grab her by the shoulders and shake her until she coughed up the truth, gave me an explanation for just taking off the way she did. We were best friends and she just walked away from it!

But as much as I wanted to ask for the truth, I wouldn't.

Because maybe I didn't want to know the answer.

Besides, what was the point? It wasn't going to change anything.

I'd moved on. There was no room left for

Charlie in my life.

Wrapping my fingers around the cold glass, I sat at the metal table opposite my high school buddy and gave her a pointed look. "Columbia's a good school. I'd be lucky to get in there."

"As long as it's what you want, then more power to you, man." She raised her glass. "To the Big Apple, and all the exciting adventures you'll have here."

It took me a second to raise my glass and tap it against hers.

Exciting adventures. Those two words didn't really feature in my life anymore. Not since Charlie left.

My throat grew thick with a mixture of longing and pain.

Being around her was a really bad idea.

I should go join that line again. It's safe there.

Safe and boring!

I gulped back the cold amber brew and gazed at my friend. She winked at me, her eyes dancing with that familiar cheer I could never resist.

Unnerved by my weakness around her, I shuffled in my seat and pointed to her camera. "So, photography. No surprises there. It's the perfect job for you."

"Yeah, well I've tried a bunch of different stuff, but I always come back to it. After high school…" Her voice cut off as her eyes darted to her glass. She started drawing patterns in the condensation, the chipper spark from her voice dying a little. "I moved to Montana for a few months, um, to stay with my aunt. She's a—"

"Nature photographer. I remember."

Charlie gave me a closed-mouth smile. "Yeah, well, she taught me everything she knew and then… Yeah, I just really loved it."

"You always loved it," I murmured.

My soft comment froze us both and we stared at each other for a minute. I didn't know what she was thinking, but my mind shot straight back to Yosemite and the summer after graduation. The one that simultaneously made and destroyed my life.

"I've never deleted one photo of you," she murmured, her eyes shining when she smiled at me. "I even kept those ones of that time you dressed up like a woman and I tried to pull off being a guy. Do you remember that?"

I forced out a snicker. "I still don't know how you talked me into that."

"We had people fooled."

"Except that old couple in the diner. Do you remember them? They were so confused."

"And then so horrified." Charlie laughed out her sentence, her voice deep with a chuckle.

The smile that lit her face was sunshine and I couldn't help joining her. "You told me you'd delete those."

"No, I didn't. I just promised to never show them to anyone." Her right eyebrow arched. "And I never have. They are reserved for my private collection, which I only pull out when I need a good belly laugh."

I grinned at the expression on her face, wondering what other photos she had in there. No doubt the ones of me diving off the high board at the community pool after she dared me. I nearly shit my pants, it was so freaking terrifying. She had her finger planted on the button and got like twenty snapshots of my fear.

I'd never heard her laugh so hard.

But that smile she gave me. That pride.

Man, I'd loved her in that moment. I'd loved her since the day I met her.

I drank another mouthful of beer, hoping it'd cool the burning inside me. The one that reminded me she was never meant to be mine.

She'd always been too wild and crazy for boring ol' me.

Sometimes her carefree nature scared me. Most of the time it drew me in.

But not anymore.

I was with the right person. Shayna was stable, settled. She liked to plan, and it was easy to just follow along with whatever she wanted. We were a good match. And she wasn't going to ditch me without a word. She wasn't one for surprises, so I never had to worry about impulsive behavior or hare-brained ideas.

It was good.

It was…safe.

Charlie licked the beer off her bottom lip, her eyes narrowing as she studied me.

"What?" My eyebrows flickered with a frown.

She pursed her lips. "You don't look happy."

I groaned and tipped my head to the sky, trying to hide how rattled I was by Charlie's perceptiveness. "I'm stuck in a snowbound airport, destined to have a crappy night's sleep on some hard plastic chairs or a dirty airport floor. Of course I'm not happy."

She snorted and shook her head. "Well, we definitely have to do something about that."

I narrowed my eyes at her. "You can't fix this one. You don't have a magic wand to get rid of the snow. You can't magically fly me home. I just have to accept the fact that things aren't going to plan."

"Or..." She leaned across the table and patted my forearm. "You could embrace the moment and think of this as an opportunity to have some fun at JFK!"

Her eyes danced with her sales pitch, her bright face reminding me of everything I'd been missing.

I scoffed and fought a smile. The eternal optimist. She hadn't changed a bit.

"I'm taking on this challenge." She pointed at me.

"What challenge?"

"To make you smile so wide it hurts your face. And to make you relax and do something...unhindered." She slapped the table and stood, running back to the bar and returning a few minutes later with tequila shots.

"No." I shook my head.

"Yes!" She grabbed my hand and gave it a quick lick before sprinkling some salt on it.

I sighed while she did the same to her own

hand. Holding out a shot glass, she gave me a bright smile. "You ready?"

I shook my head but took the glass anyway.

"Okay. One, two, three." She laughed, licked her hand and then threw the shot back.

I did the same and winced at the burning sensation down my throat. Grabbing the lime wedge, I sucked it, then stuck out my tongue.

Charlie laughed and pointed at me. "You're so cute."

"You're so annoying." I wiped my mouth with a paper napkin and was sure she was about to say, "Another one?"

But she didn't.

Because "Have Fun Go Mad" started playing through the speakers, which rushed us both back to the homecoming dance of our junior year. The song was unknown to most, but we'd always been eclectic with our tastes and we discovered the song on a British pop playlist. Charlie fell in love with it and was determined to have it play at homecoming. She took the song on a flash drive and hounded the DJ until he capitulated and played it right near the end.

She pointed at me, her lips rounding into a big O, her face lighting up like a Fourth of July fireworks display.

"No way!" She jumped from her seat, her hips swaying in a sexy move that cut off my air supply for a second. "Do you remember this? Homecoming!"

I nodded and averted my gaze, noticing the

people at the table next to us giving Charlie an odd look.

"Come on, sit down." I nodded at the chair.

"How? It's 'Have Fun Go Mad.' This is epic! We gotta dance, man." She started mouthing the words, her blue-tipped hair flying out as she spun and raised her arms.

She was oblivious to the crowd of people around us, the curious glances, the laughter and pointing fingers.

"Freaking shameless," I muttered under my breath, but I couldn't help but smile that she remembered all the words and was killing it in the small space.

The chorus kicked in and she winked at the lady next to her. The older woman grinned and shook her head while Charlie danced around her and started wooing the crowd.

By the time the second chorus kicked in, people around me were clapping in time, some were cheering, and others had started singing along.

I got it—Charlie Watson was damn impossible to resist.

She laughed and worked her way back to me. Her eyes were bright and alluring, and I knew I was toast before she'd even reached our table.

When she held out her hand, I took it.

When she pulled me to my feet, I stood.

And when the words kicked in again, I mouthed them right along with her, transporting myself back to the high school gymnasium and those times in my life when all that mattered was squeezing every ounce of joy from the moment.

FOUR

CHARLIE

Nixon smiled. He danced. He laughed.

Mission completed.

But then the song ended and his phone buzzed again. Within two seconds, everything I'd achieved was flushed down the toilet by one simple text.

I have no idea what it said, but it made his lips press together and he gave me this sad smile before grabbing his bag.

"I gotta go back down and check the whole flight status thing."

Then he just walked off without so much as a "See ya later."

Very rude.

Very un-Nixon.

I grabbed my stuff and raced after him.

When I caught up, he kind of flinched and forced a tight smile.

Shit. I wanted to turn back time.

I never could, and hell, even if I were able to…would I choose to play it differently?

I'd walked away because that was what he needed me to do.

He may not have realized it at the time, but I'd been convinced.

And look at him four years later, going off to law school and doing great…the way he deserved to be.

But I couldn't shake that horrible, ugly feeling in my chest. The one that reminded me of how much I'd lost…and how I'd probably hurt him.

I wanted to make it up to him. Try to somehow amend the damage I'd done, so that even if we never saw each other again, his final memories of me would be good…happy.

We got to the line, only to find it had grown.

Nixon swore under his breath, scratching the back of his head and glancing down at his phone.

I was tempted to look over his arm and see what he was typing, but I didn't want to cross that line. It was no doubt his parents hassling him for not being where he should be, and that would only piss me off.

Frickin' control freaks!

I clenched my jaw as a flash of hate fire burned

through my chest. But then it was stolen by the logic that had driven me away in the first place. It reminded me that even though they pissed me off, they always had Nixon at the front of their minds. They wanted what was best for him.

And I'd let them win because maybe they were right.

My idea of happiness was different from theirs.

Confusion made my face bunch as the war I'd been waging for years swelled up inside me again.

"Shit." Nixon breathed the word as he slid the phone into his pocket. "Come on, snow. Melt already."

I studied his expression and saw the telltale signs of pressure. I always hated that look on his face. It didn't suit him, and it wasn't half as beautiful as those carefree smiles.

I wanted to help, make it all better for him. Touching his arm, I ignored the way he flinched and gave him a light squeeze before dropping my hand.

"You need to get home, don't you?"

"Yeah." He sighed. "But I'm stuck, and I can't give her a definitive answer of when I'll be back."

His mother had always been a stickler for timing. She worried too much.

I tried to remind myself why she was inclined to act that way. After what happened to Reagan, she'd poured every ounce of her love and devotion into her husband and son. She'd never survive losing her golden boy.

I worked my jaw to the side and thought about

the woman with her dark brown hair, always styled in a sleek bob. Her manicured nails—always French, never color. Her brown eyes that used to study me like I was some kind of biohazard that would destroy her only child's life. I was dangerous.

Probably because I reminded her of Reagan.

I was basically the only thing Nixon ever disobeyed them on. Not that they outright forbid him to see me. They wouldn't want to get their precious son off-side.

My mind flashed with a memory I hadn't dredged up in years. Mr. Holloway's steely voice, the determination on his face, the bright warning that told me I had no chance of getting what I wanted.

I shuddered and shoved it back where it belonged—in the pile of *I can't spend any more time thinking about that!*

Whether I wanted to turn back time or not, I couldn't.

But I *could* do something about the present. I was standing next to the only person I'd ever considered a best friend. He was upset, and I wanted to take that pressure off his shoulders.

My mind hummed with different ideas, things he could say to appease his mother, but I kept coming back to the first thought that popped into my mind…

Road trip.

Sounded crazy, but it had a lot going for it. One, it'd get Nixon on the move, heading home to LA just the way mother dearest wanted. Secondly, it'd give me a chance to spend a little more time with him…a chance to make up for what I'd done. A chance to leave behind a better memory.

Nibbling my lip, I looked down at my purple boots while doubts tried to yank the idea from my mind.

But…screw it.

I wanted a freaking road trip with my best friend!

Puffing out a breath, I glanced at Nixon and blurted, "You know you could always drive home."

He shot me an incredulous look. "Drive? That'll take a week!"

"Well, not if you drive really long days. I can be your buddy, and we could take turns. I'm confident we can punch it out in four days flat."

"By then I could have flown home."

"True." I raised my finger. "But it'll be way funner. Because road trips are always fun. And then you can tell—" I pointed at the phone. "—that you're doing everything in your power to get home. That'll work like a charm. You know it will." I leaned into his side with my best smile. "And come on, Nix. Do you seriously want to spend the next couple of days at the airport while you wait for the weather to clear?"

I spread my arms wide and indicated the overloaded seats piled with luggage and grumpy travelers.

His expression was droll and adorable. "You

want to rent a car?"

"That's what I'm saying." I nodded. "It's got to be better than hard plastic chairs or a dirty airport floor."

His eyebrows dipped but he didn't say anything, so I kept on with the sell.

"Look, if your mom gets antsy about the new plan, we can drop off the car halfway home and fly from there. Seriously, it's no big deal. Let's just play it by ear."

"Play it by ear," he muttered. "Yeah, that's gonna fly."

"The point is no one is flying anywhere, so let's drive, baby." I wiggled my eyebrows and started chanting. "Road trip. Road trip."

FIVE

NIXON

She was chanting.

And I was done for.

It didn't make sense to drive.

It was crazy.

Charlie thought I was texting my mom. I didn't have the heart to tell her about Shayna yet. I mean, I would…if I agreed to her insane road trip idea.

She *did* have a point about actually doing something rather than just sitting around.

It'd be a hard sell to Shayna though. She'd be confused, maybe annoyed. But if I worded it right, I could probably win her over. She was a lot like my mom that way.

Scratching the back of my neck, I glanced down at Charlie. The exact opposite of the girl I'd ended up with.

Maybe hanging out with her for a few days would remind me why it was so good that I'd moved on, found someone trustworthy and safe. Sure, Shayna was a lot like my mother and yes, sometimes I glimpsed into my future and had a little freak-out. But Shayna wasn't going to ditch me without a goodbye.

And she wasn't going to drag me on some crazy adventure only to leave me heartbroken.

Yeah, spending a little time with Charlie would be good. It'd be a chance to remind myself of everything I had, and maybe help me find some closure.

We'd have a couple of days to hang out and reminisce…and then I could let her go.

I kind of needed that before I moved into the next phase of my life anyway.

"So?" Charlie looked at me expectantly.

I grimaced and pulled out my phone.

Shayna had already replied to my last text.

I know it's not your fault. I'm just disappointed.

I'll look forward to seeing you when you get back. I'm sure I'll have plenty of exciting things to share. Without you around, the girls and I can go a little cray-cray.

The rest of the message was emojis—funny faces, love hearts. Then she sent a gif of three girls laughing together. I smiled at the screen. It was the perfect choice.

Shayna and I lived with her two best friends—Mimi and Harper. It wasn't all bad. They were nice girls, but sometimes the smell of perfume and nail polish, the giggles and the incessant girl-talk, got a little too much.

Delaying my return by a few days would actually be kind of nice.

The cheerful gif gave me hope that Shayna would be okay with the road trip. I'd just let her know *after* I was on my way.

Pressing my lips together, I texted back.

Thanks for understanding. I'm doing everything in my power to get home to you.

I shoved in a love heart because I knew she liked it, then slid my phone away and did a slow circle. "Where are the rental counters? Will they even be open?"

"Yes! That's my boy!" Charlie pumped her fist and pointed to a sign on the wall. "There's only one way to find out, my friend." She jumped on my back before I could stop her.

I laughed, loving how familiar it felt. How many memories rushed back.

I'd piggybacked her through the school corridors. She'd sing and laugh in my ear, or tell me some funny story from the couple of classes we didn't have together.

She made high school excellent.

She'd been my best friend.

And there was something very liberating about hanging out with her again.

I slid her off my back and softened the move with a grin. I'd have to keep reminding myself *why* I was agreeing to her impulsive road trip.

It was for closure.

So we could say the goodbye we should have said four years ago.

SIX

CHARLIE

I paced behind Nixon while he signed the rest of the paperwork so he could drive the car too. It was costing a freaking bomb with extra fees and insurance, but his credit card could handle it. He may have been twenty-two, but his overbearing parents still supplied all his needs.

Shaking my head with a wry smile, I couldn't deny a small burst of triumph. If only his dad knew that Nixon was racking up a hefty bill so he could spend some time with me.

Essentially his father was funding a road trip that he would be against in so many ways.

I wondered if time had managed to change his mind at all, if he was still anti-Charlie with the same vehemence he used to be.

My forehead wrinkled. His son had become the man he'd wanted him to be. I'd helped make that happen, so it wasn't like he could hold that against me.

He'd still find something to hate. I rolled my eyes and tried not to think about it.

Nixon's dad wasn't in New York, so he couldn't go shitting all over our plans.

A smile tugged at my lips when I glanced at the back of Nixon's head.

A road trip with Nix.

It was like a dream come true. The chance I'd been waiting for.

A chance I didn't deserve, but still…I was taking it.

All those years of pining and regret.

I wanted to tell him the truth, give him a reason to forgive me. But I wouldn't do that. The truth was too destructive. Four years ago, I left for a reason. And even though that reason hurt, I…

With a shake of my head, I kept pacing.

I didn't want to taint the trip with serious conversations and ugly truths. I just wanted to live in the moment and have some fun.

I'd make this the best frickin' road trip Nixon had ever been on.

We'd hang out, have a good time, walk down memory lane with a few laughs and tons of music. It was just what we needed, a way to set things right again.

My phone started playing "Thunderbirds Are Go" by Busted. As usual I took my time answering it so I could enjoy the song first, and ended up singing the line about Tracy Island instead of saying "hello" when I lifted the phone to my ear.

"Ugh, you seriously need to change your ringtone."

I grinned at the sound of my roommate's voice. "Not a chance, Flissy. The Thunderbirds will forever be cool."

"You're unbelievable."

"I think the word you're looking for is adorable."

Fliss's snort turned into a giggle. "I'm just calling to see if you're okay. The news said flights out of JFK are not in the cards tonight."

"Yeah, I was gonna call. You don't have to pick me up at an unreasonable hour of the morning anymore."

"And I love you for that."

"Why? Because it means you can spend the night with Flick?"

"He's actually right here, and now that I won't be waking him with my alarm, I think he might just stay."

"As long as his naked ass doesn't touch the couch again, I'm cool with that."

"You got home like three hours before you said you would."

I rolled my eyes as we replayed the same argument we'd been having for months. "Catching you guys is not even the point. His ass cheeks were on the couch where I sit to watch TV and do things that normal people do on a couch."

"Everybody has sex on a couch." Fliss's tone was dry and unshakeable.

I frowned. "Not everybody."

She groaned. "How many times do we have to say sorry for this one?"

"Until Flick buys us a new couch."

She snorted and relayed my message.

"Not happening." Flick's shout was distant but made me smile.

I loved the guy, and I was so happy he and Fliss had lasted as long as they had. The amount they bickered and "discussed" stuff was unreal, but they just kept coming back to each other.

In the nearly three years they'd been dating, they'd broken up four times, but never for more than a month. They were currently on their longest stretch and things were going well enough that I couldn't see a breakup anywhere in the near future.

"Anyway," I brought the conversation back on point, "I've decided to drive back."

Fliss sputtered on whatever she was drinking. "Drive back?"

"Yeah, I um, found a driving buddy and we think we can make it back in like four days."

Fliss didn't answer right away. Never a good sign.

I forced a smile when Nixon caught my eye. He pointed to the men's bathroom and I gave him a thumbs-up.

"Driving buddy," Fliss eventually muttered. "Please tell me this isn't one of your spontaneous *I've just made a new best friend* moments, and tomorrow I'll be reading about how the police found your body in a ditch outside of New York."

"Okay. You're allowed to call me crazy, but not stupid. It's an old buddy of mine from high school."

I could picture Fliss's eyes narrowing. "Who?"

"Um…" I scratched the side of my nose and looked down at my purple boots. "His name's Nixon. You don't know him."

"Nixon? As in the guy you never got over?"

My eyes rounded. Shit. When had I even told her about that?

"I… That… I'm over him. I'm not… We were never a couple."

"Yet you've always been in love with him. I've done enough shots with you to know that much."

I gritted my teeth, cursing my drunken mouth. "We're just driving back to LA together. It's no big deal."

"O-kay." She drew out the word, basically telling me she thought I was full of shit.

I huffed. "You don't believe me."

"No. I think you're going to end up falling in love with him all over again and you'll get back to LA a sad, pathetic mess."

My nostrils flared as I gripped the phone, and for a fleeting second I wished I'd never moved in with Kelly's sister-in-law. "Thanks for your encouragement, roomie."

"Yeah, well Maestro and I will be available for comfort cuddles as soon as you get back."

As if agreeing with her, Maestro barked in the background. His tail was probably going nuts.

I bit back a smile and managed a clipped, "You suck."

"Yet I love you enough to say it."

I rolled my eyes. "Come on, Fliss. This decision is not all bad. It'll give me a chance to—"

"What if he has a girlfriend?" She cut me off with a thought that felt like rusting copper in my belly—a green, toxic ache that I had to douse with serious amounts of logic.

"This isn't about hooking up or anything. I'm not…" I sighed, not sure what my answer even was. "I just want to spend a little time with him. Somehow make it right."

Fliss only knew part of the story. At least I thought that was all she knew.

I left Nixon with no explanation. That's all I could admit to. Saying more only made me cry and I hated doing that.

"Okay," Fliss whispered. "Just don't do anything impulsive, okay? Your life is good right now. You've been in the same place for nearly a year. That's like a record for you. And his life is probably settled and awesome. So, you know, be careful."

I pursed my lips, scrambling for a light way to end the conversation. I didn't want her worrying about me.

"You know, for someone who dates a rock star,

you're extremely boring."

"I think the word you're looking for is sensible."

"Boring."

"Sensible."

I gave up with a huff. If Fliss was anything, she was stubborn, and I'd never win a fight like that with her.

She giggled in my ear. "Drive safe, Chuck. I love you."

"Love you too," I muttered before hanging up.

I slipped the phone into my bag just as Nixon came out of the bathroom. His smile was sweet, the way it always had been, and I walked toward it…hope, excitement and maybe just a touch of fear fluttering in my ribcage.

I was about to get the redemption I'd been hoping for since the day I took off to Montana.

SEVEN

NIXON

Driving out of NYC was slow going. Not only was it midnight by the time we pulled out of the airport, but there was also still a light snow falling and I wasn't used to driving in those conditions. I gripped the wheel tight enough for my fingers to ache, driving at a snail's pace along the slushy roads.

It was insane. I was in a car with my long-lost love, driving through the snow while my disappointed girlfriend waited for me, clueless to what I was really doing.

You're such an idiot, man.

I ignored the derogatory voice in my head and concentrated on the road.

Thanks to snow plows, the highway was pretty clear, but I still took my sweet time while Charlie rabbited on about how pretty the snow looked in the streetlights. Only she could make something beautiful out of a nuisance like snow.

I leaned forward and glanced up through the windshield like she told me to. White flakes spun and danced in the light beams, creating a magic that you couldn't find in LA. My lips twitched with a smile.

Charlie, totally inspired, lowered her window and snapped shots using different shutter speeds. The couple of times I glanced at her she was staring at the digital display on the back of her camera with this excited grin on her face. It made the frigid breeze she was letting in easier to bear.

Her smile warmed me, making it impossible to say, "Can you put up the window, please?"

Eventually there was a click and a whir as the window slowly shut out the cold. I focused on the road and getting us safely through to Pennsylvania while Charlie hummed and fiddled with her favorite toy.

I'd always loved how creative she was.

Before we officially met, I'd known her as the girl with the camera. The artsy weird one who spent most of her time looking at everything through a lens. She didn't have many friends. She was one of those *friends with everybody* kind of people. Always talking to someone, but never really attached.

It wasn't until we connected over an iPod at the start of junior year that her status changed. We became an inseparable duo—Nixon and Charlie. Charlie and Nix. It soon got shortened to Chix, which I didn't particularly love, but it made Charlie laugh so I never said anything.

Leaning her head back against the headrest, Charlie let out a loud yawn, which set me off.

"Man, I'm tired," I murmured, rubbing my eyes and checking the clock. We'd been driving for over two hours.

"Yeah, me too." Charlie gazed out the windshield.

The snow had stopped falling, the inky night sky an endless mass in front of us. The state highway was well lit, but driving at night when tired was never the safest way to go.

"Why don't we find a truck stop or something. We can catch a few Zs in the car. Even just a couple of hours to recharge the batteries."

"Sounds good to me." Charlie smiled.

I pointed at my phone. "Find us something, will ya?"

I told her my pin number and she unlocked the phone. Thankfully my messages weren't up. I didn't really want her seeing Shayna's name. I didn't know why. I guess I still wasn't ready to bring my girlfriend into the equation. I would eventually, but not when I was running on fumes.

After some sleep and a coffee, there was a chance I'd find the courage to raise it.

I had to find the courage.

As tempting as it was to pretend that Shayna didn't exist for the next few days, it'd be an asshole thing to do. I didn't want it tainting my time with Charlie, but it was my reality. I had a girlfriend…and Charlie needed to know.

About thirty minutes later, somewhere near Allentown, we pulled into a truck stop and parked away from the 24-hour diner. The weather in Pennsylvania was pretty clear. Yanking a jacket out of my bag, I passed it to Charlie so she wouldn't get cold. She hesitated before taking it, her eyes misting with a look that told me I was a sweet guy and maybe she'd missed me.

I wanted to scoff and ask her why the hell she'd left then, but I pressed my lips together and rolled away from her, trying to get comfy on the seat. Even though I'd pushed it back as far as it could go, it was no bed.

Sleep captured me eventually, but it didn't last more than a couple of hours. It was impossible to reach complete oblivion with the uncomfortable position and the constant coming and going of trucks.

Eventually Charlie sat up with a huff and muttered, "I'm getting coffee."

I glanced at my watch and noted the time — 5:30 a.m.

I dragged my butt out of the car and we had a silent breakfast inside the diner. We were both too tired to chat. But by the time we hit the road again, our bellies filled with food and caffeine running through our veins, we felt a little better.

Charlie offered to drive, but I wanted to keep going. I liked the excuse of a wheel in my hand and a windshield to look out of. If I just sat in the passenger seat, I'd end up staring at her, studying the curve of her cheek and the way her blue hair rested on her breasts.

She'd always had great breasts—34 C.

The only reason I knew that was because she made me go bra shopping with her once. For a girl with her tiny frame, her breasts were pretty decent. Decent and perfect. That's what I'd told her when she was lamenting the fact that her boobs felt enormous and she hated them.

The smile on her face after I told her what I thought would be permanently burned into my memory.

I cleared my throat and shuffled in my seat. Charlie was messing around with the stereo while she sucked on a blueberry lollipop and tried to find some decent music to play. Every radio station was either ads, talking, or a total bust on music awesomeness.

In the end she huffed and pulled out her phone, then scrambled around in her bag until she yanked out a connection cable.

Plugging it in, she got some music going off her Spotify playlist before nestling it into a cup holder. With a satisfied smile, she leaned her head back and looked at me.

"In Too Deep" by Sum 41 blasted through the car and I couldn't help but smile. Man, that brought back some memories. We used to rock out to that song all the time, especially during finals. Charlie would sing it, her face awash with panic as we walked toward the testing rooms.

I'd wrap my arm around her and tell her she'd be fine.

I don't know if she ever believed me.

But she graduated, and her grades were good enough to get into community college. She'd talked about attending one near UCLA until her plans changed and she just disappeared.

I gripped the wheel, clenching my jaw against that feeling. It was like dry ash in my throat and burning bile in my stomach. I felt like I'd lost my life the day I found out she'd ditched all our plans and taken off.

Charlie pulled the lollipop out of her mouth and licked her shiny blue lips.

"So, I never asked you last night. How'd you manage to convince your parents that driving back was all good? I saw you texting and then you turned for the counter. Surely they were pissed."

My lips rose into a half smile. She still thought I'd been texting my parents back and forth. I kept up the illusion and murmured, "I just said I was doing everything I could to get home. I'll no doubt get another text soon and I'll reply with what I'm doing, saying I couldn't sit around in New York. Driving would be a nice chance for me to unwind before…" I glanced at Charlie and swallowed.

"Before what?"

I shrugged, not wanting to go there. "Before the

hard stuff really kicks in."

She slowly put the lollipop back into her mouth, her eyes narrowing as she studied my profile. "You're being vague."

I have to be vague, dammit!

I couldn't go there. I could *not* get the words out of my mouth.

I sighed and scratched the back of my head. "You know, the hard stuff. The last chunk before law school. It's going to be crazy, and there's no guarantees I'll get into Columbia."

She snorted. "You'll get into Columbia. Come on, Nix. There's nothing you can't do."

Except keep you.

The thought came out of nowhere and kind of surprised me with its fervor.

I gritted my teeth and kept my eyes ahead.

"You know, I thought you had your heart set on journalism. The whole lawyer thing kind of surprises me."

I shrugged and wondered why my throat suddenly felt so thick. "I took a few journalism classes in my first year, but…" I blinked and shook my head. "Law's a good choice for my future. Plenty of job opportunities and potential in a career like that."

Shit. Did I just parrot my dad?

"Yeah, for sure. If it makes you happy, then go for it."

I turned away and rolled my eyes. Why did she always have to go on about being happy, like it was the sole purpose for living?

She had been my happy and she'd left, making me miserable. I'd learned not to put so much stock in happiness. Contentment was way more important.

"So, are you still writing?" she asked.

I blinked and checked out the landscape to my left. The sun was rising behind us, the golden light hitting the clouds and turning them all shades of yellow, orange and pink.

I checked the rearview mirror and distracted Charlie with it.

She looked over her shoulder and gasped, then yanked out her camera. I was given a short reprieve from having to admit that since she left, my passion for the written word had kind of died. I just couldn't get into it. All those classes had done was remind me of everything I'd wanted to do with Charlie. In the end I quit them and started taking classes that had nothing to do with writing. Dad suggested a bunch of different things and I just kind of followed along until I found myself heading for law. It wasn't so bad. I didn't know what the hell else I wanted to do, and I liked that following in his footsteps made him so proud.

Once the clicking was done and Charlie had checked out what she'd taken, she tucked her camera away and asked again, "So, the writing. You still doing it?"

I shook my head, unable to fight a glum smile. "I just don't have time. Classes keep me way busier than I thought they would."

Her forehead crinkled with sadness, her lips

dipping into a soft frown. "Bummer. You were so good. I used to love reading your stuff. Those articles you wrote for the school paper were genius. Hell, you *were* the school paper, dude."

I grinned. "Yeah, I remember. You took the photos and I turned them into a story."

"I know that probably made us super nerds, but I felt so incredibly cool and empowered."

Leaning forward with a carefree laugh, I tapped the wheel with my hand and enjoyed a few memories. Our small class in Mr. Sheffield's cluttered room. We'd sit at our computers for hours. I'd been appointed chief editor and I put Charlie in charge of photography. Mae, Aubrey and Walnut (shit, I can't even remember his real name!) were reporters, Chen and Izzy were the proofreaders and the girl with the bright red curls was in charge of layout.

"Who was the layout girl again?"

"Oh, Strawberry Shortcake." Charlie nodded. "She was a cool chick."

"What was her real name?"

Charlie paused, her eyes narrowing before her forehead wrinkled. "Susanna?" The way her voice pitched told me she was plucking the name out of thin air.

I snickered and shook my head at how useless we were.

Putting together the monthly school paper had been one of my favorite things to do. Man, we'd had some sway at the school the week before publication. All the jocks wanted to make sure their names were in there, and the drama kids demanded we write ad nauseam about their plays. The principal was always concerned that we didn't take the whole "free speech" thing too seriously. And our advisors just wanted to make sure we got the damned thing out by our deadline each month.

We always did. And it was freaking awesome.

"Hopefully I'll get back to it one day," I murmured.

I couldn't imagine it. Between studying, Shayna and my parents, I didn't really have time for myself. Besides, my heart hadn't been in it. According to my parents, journalism wasn't a secure path to take. They were going to let me give it a try, but I knew they wanted something more stable for me. I was prepared to push and fight for it, but when Charlie left like she did, all the zeal went right out of me, and it was easier to just go along with what they suggested.

Our plans had been so huge that summer. Charlie and I spent hours talking about what we'd do.

And then it all fell apart.

I glanced at my friend, fighting a mixture of anger and despair. I wanted to hate her for changing my life so suddenly, but then I couldn't. Because she was Charlie. And hating her was impossible.

"So, how are the travel plans coming?"

Her smile was tight. "Still working on it. Saving. You know how it is."

"You *were* going to travel the world."

"And I still am," she snapped, then softened her defensive tone with a grin. "I'll get there. One day. I will. I still want to see every country on this planet if I can."

She stared at the dash, her lips twitching into a frown.

"You know, I always thought you'd gone without me. When you first left after the summer, and then never came back, I couldn't help but wonder if you'd just…flown away." I flicked my fingers through the air, trying to sound like the idea didn't kill me.

Charlie's face crumpled with a look I couldn't determine. For a second I thought she was about to cry, but then she drew in a slow breath and looked out her window. "I went to my aunt's place in Montana."

"Yeah, I know," I mumbled.

"She taught me a bunch of awesome stuff, really set me on the right path, you know?"

"So you didn't go to college at all, then?"

"I, um…" She looked down and started tracing the checkers on her pants. "I enrolled for the second semester, but I hated it, so I dropped out to pursue photography."

"But still no travel."

"A bit. I mean, I've gone up and down the West Coast and back to Montana again. Just working different jobs and…" She shrugged. "But I've been in LA for nearly a year. A friend of mine lost her roommate so I stepped up, and the feeble business I started three years ago really picked up once I stopped moving around. It's a good way to make some money…so I can travel. Because I'll get there, Nix. I'm definitely going." She looked at me, her hazel eyes bright with determination…and something else. I didn't know what it was, but there was something deeper going on in that gaze. Because I was driving, I couldn't look at her long enough to figure it out.

Facing the road again, I concentrated on getting us back to LA safely.

Because that's where my real life was.

A girl who'd never break my heart was waiting for me.

And I had to get back to her before the girl beside me unearthed all the buried dreams and hopes I'd been squashing in order to survive.

EIGHT

CHARLIE

I couldn't believe Nixon called me out on the whole travel thing.

And I couldn't believe he wasn't writing anymore!

That was a travesty.

He was amazing. The guy knew how to make the most boring information sound fascinating. He would have made such a great reporter…or a travel writer.

That was the plan, way back then. I'd take the photos, he'd write about them, and we'd publish books about our adventures around the world.

It could have been so epic.

But then I destroyed it.

For his own security.

I wanted so badly to explain that to him, but I couldn't. How did I admit what had happened? The repercussions were huge, and so destructive.

No, I'd done the right thing. I just wished that it *felt* like I'd done the right thing. Because as I sat there in that car, listening to his sad voice and enduring the sad conversation that basically implied neither of us were doing what we wanted with our lives…I had to wonder if I'd made a huge mistake.

As if to amplify my doubts, "Break Me Down" popped up on my playlist.

The only words I could hear throughout the entire song were "I'm yours."

It hurt because it was true.

I was Nixon's. I always would be.

I'd never wanted any other boyfriend. Even though Chix never officially dated, we had both wanted to. That summer proved it. We finally overcame our fears of ruining our friendship.

But then I had to walk away.

And I'd never moved on.

I'd tried—gone on a bunch of different dates, but I could never make it anything more than a night of fun. If my date got too handsy or serious I'd back away in a flash. No guy had ever compared to Nixon. We'd had depth that no one could match.

So I kept it light and if a guy ever tried to fall in

love with me, I'd cut him off or move away.

That's what you're so good at, right?

Running away.

The thought was dark and brutal.

Crossing my arms, I rested my boots on the dash and glared out the window.

I didn't need a stupid boyfriend to make me happy.

Stealing a glimpse at Nixon's handsome face, I knew that was total bullshit.

I mean, I was happy. But I was smart enough to know that being with Nixon always made me happier.

The thought that maybe he'd moved on and found joy with someone else shot through me. It was like a freaking speargun to the chest, and I didn't want to know.

But then Fliss's warnings echoed in the back of my mind and I was compelled to blurt, "You dating anyone?"

Nixon stilled, then gave me a quick glance. "Yeah. I am."

The words were acid in my ears but I forced a smile. "Is it serious?"

"It could be heading that way, yeah." His jaw worked to the side, his eyes trained on the road ahead.

I didn't know what to say. I figured screaming *"How the hell could you move on when I haven't stopped loving you for one second?"* wouldn't fly, so I swallowed the glass shards in my throat and murmured, "Good on you, man. She pretty?"

"Yeah." His lips twitched with a smile.

"What does she do?"

"She's in human resources. She got an assistant's job last year and is working towards a managerial role."

"Wow. Cool." I bobbed my head, kind of lost for words. Human resources? A manager? That didn't seem like Nixon's type.

Because it wasn't like me at all.

I'd go out of my mind working in an office job like that.

I squeezed my eyes shut and turned away from Nix.

Was I seriously arrogant enough to think I'd be the only girl he'd ever like?

Disappointment spiked through me. He'd moved on. He had a freaking human resources girlfriend who no doubt wore heels and fitted skirts with matching jackets—the exact opposite of me.

Hurt wasn't a big enough word to describe what was happening to my heart.

But anger overrode the emotion.

What had I expected?

I'd left him with no explanation. Of course he was going to fucking move on!

"You?"

I jerked at Nixon's question and spun back to face him. "Me what?"

"Do you have a boyfriend?" His voice was deep and thick, his Adam's apple sticking out when he swallowed.

I bobbed my head before I could stop myself. I didn't know why I did that. Maybe I wanted to save face, I'm not sure. But I did. I lied.

"Yeah. I mean, sort of." I captured one of my blue curls and wound it around my pinky finger. "It's been a bit on again, off again. We're currently on a breather, but who knows, I'll probably end up marrying the guy." I laughed and pinched my lower lip, looking out my window so I didn't have to see Nixon's face.

He was probably happy for me, dammit!

He'd moved on.

He had a girlfriend.

A beautiful one who made him smile. She no doubt had perfect legs and perky little breasts that meant she could wear anything and look smoking hot.

Once again, I crossed my arms over my chest and looked out the window.

I never should have suggested the road trip. It was a terrible idea.

But I couldn't blurt out the fact that I wanted to travel across the country with him to try and recreate what we'd had that summer.

The thought made me still.

Really? Is that really what I'm trying to do?

Make amends and *go back to where we never should have left off?*

Grinding my teeth together, I kept my eyes trained on the scenery flashing past.

You're a hopeless dreamer, Chuck.

Nixon had a girlfriend.

My eyes burned.

She was waiting for him in LA.

Shit, I thought he'd been worried about his parents, but it was no doubt his girlfriend he'd been texting.

She better be damn amazing.

And she better treat Nixon like a fucking king.

My nostrils flared, my jaw trembling as I fought the emotion inside of me.

If I didn't do something soon, I was going to explode.

Thankfully music saved my ass like it always did.

The guitar riff for "Raise Your Glass" came on and I rushed for the volume, cranking it up and throwing all my emotion into singing.

Nixon cracked up—a loud, surprising burst of sound.

I whipped around to look at him. His smile was so damn adorable. "What's so funny?"

"Do you remember that time you performed this at the school karaoke competition?"

A hot memory flashed through my mind and I couldn't help a sheepish grin.

"I thought Principal Maclean was gonna burst a blood vessel. You got the entire school up and dancing like crazy people. It was fantastic." He shook his head, quietly snickering like he loved my antics.

He was the only one who ever had.

Which was why I'd always be his.

Because he was the guy who'd put up with my

shit and still love me at the end of the day.

I lurched for my phone and skipped back to the beginning, needing to throw myself into an uninterrupted performance. I needed some way to release the pressure inside.

Pumping up the volume a few more notches, I went for it, banging my head and singing the words at the top of my lungs.

And Nixon joined me.

Because we were Chix.

NINE

NIXON

She was so wild.

Watching her blue hair fly out the window as she leaned out and sang "Raise Your Glass" to the passing traffic made something in my chest pop. An explosion of affection that I only ever felt around her.

Sometimes she reminded me of Reagan—all happiness and sunshine.

But she had a sweetness that Reagan lacked. My sister was set on beating the world, proving that nothing could best her. She was a feisty adrenaline junkie.

But Charlie…she just wanted to have fun. No conflict. No tears. Just good times and laughter.

She was an escape from my mundane life.

I'd been convinced she was my ticket out.

But I'd been wrong.

My throat swelled and I stopped singing, focusing back on the road and my journey home. I had what I needed waiting for me in LA. Shayna had to remain my focus.

Pressing the gas, I pushed a little over the speed limit and kept powering forward.

The rest of the day was used up with singing and harmless conversation. We talked a lot about music—the new stuff we liked, bands we'd been listening to. Her taste was still as varied as always. She took me through her different playlists and when we compared, we had basically all the same music between us.

The hours ticked by while I learned more about photography and how to capture the best light. We did a few miles of selfies, her making me laugh while I drove.

She asked me about college but I brushed over as much as I could. It was so boring compared to everything she said. I didn't want to dull the moment.

I didn't really get talking until the conversation veered toward books and I was able to go on about the only escape I had left in my life. I read every night before I slept. It was the only way I could tune out and relax.

Charlie listened with interest, her nose

wrinkling and her smile growing as I described all the different places I'd been in my imagination.

We then started creating a story of our own, bouncing one crazy idea off another until we were cracking up with laughter over the young executive who had somehow found himself lost in the Amazon rainforest with nothing more than an umbrella and a briefcase containing a mysterious red bra.

Charlie's laughter floated around me and we both stopped talking for a while, giggling to ourselves as we no doubt pictured the same image.

The conversation eased off and we cruised along to the music. It wasn't awkward. If anything, it was like lying down on a bed of soft pillows—comfortable and easy.

It was nearly supper time when we drove into Lexington, Kentucky. I was happy to keep going, but Charlie was driving and she pulled into the first motel we passed.

Cutting the engine, she turned to me and said, "I'm done. I know we could probably keep going, but here looks good. We can grab a pizza, watch a movie, and sleep in a decent bed."

"Well, a bed anyway," I snickered, looking at the motel with its flickering neon sign. It wasn't dark enough to hide the dirty plaster or chipped paint around the window frames.

"It'll do," Charlie muttered, pushing the door open.

Pulling out my phone, I sent an update text to Shayna. In the call we'd had over lunchtime, she made me promise to keep her posted on my progress. She was actually taking the road trip thing really well. I'd even told her I was traveling with an old high school buddy and she thought it was great…probably because she didn't realize Chuck was actually a girl.

I winced as I punched Send, guilt niggling my insides. I hadn't exactly lied. People did call Charlie "Chuck" sometimes. Shayna had made the gender assumption on her own. And she seriously had nothing to worry about. Charlie and I were barely friends anymore. This was just a final send-off. Kind of like a mini high school reunion.

Grabbing my bag, I followed Charlie into reception and was greeted by a short lady with wrinkled chain-smoker lips and bright red hair.

"How y'all doin'?" Her voice was bored and monotone. She really didn't give a shit how we were doing.

Charlie put on an extra bright grin and leaned against the counter. "Great, thanks. Can we grab a room, please?"

"Two." I raised two fingers and stepped up to the counter.

"Two?" Charlie made a face. "It'll be so much cheaper if we share."

"It'll be so inappropriate if we do."

Resting her fist on her hip, she gave me a dry glare. "I'm not planning on jumping your bones, if that makes you feel better." She turned to the receptionist and huffed. "Can we just have a room with two beds, please?"

The woman pursed her lips, our argument obviously entertaining her. She looked between us, the edge of her mouth twitching. I clenched my jaw and didn't put up a fight when Charlie dropped her credit card down for a deposit on the room and started filling in the little form.

The receptionist handed me a key and I took it with a tight smile.

The room was up the stairs and to the right. Charlie didn't say much as I unlocked the door. My heart was thumping double time when we stepped into the musty room.

The bed covers were floral, the carpet stained beige. An ancient-looking TV sat in the corner and there was a tear in the sheer curtains covering the windows. I flicked on the light, then closed the thin drapes. I'd never liked that fishbowl effect, and I wasn't keen on the passing traffic looking in through our window.

Charlie dumped her bag on the bed next to the bathroom and smiled at me. "This isn't too bad. It doesn't feel like one of those rent-by-the-hour places, anyway." She wiggled her eyebrows, then turned to look in the bathroom. "Let's hope the shower's okay."

I nodded while she unzipped her bag. The first thing she pulled out was her phone. She got some music playing and set it down on the bedside cabinet. "Dreaming Alone" gently played in the background while she hunted for more stuff. She flung a pair of blue pajama pants with bright orange stars over her shoulder, then hugged her toiletry bag to her chest.

"Once I'm clean, we should order a pizza and play cards or something. You know…" She shrugged. "For old time's sake."

I caught her eye and we both stilled.

It was an awkward moment.

Cards.

The music playing on her phone.

It took me back to Yosemite.

The song somehow crescendoed, swirling around me until I was lost in a fog of memories that made it hurt to breathe.

Charlie's wide eyes glassed over and I knew she was back there too.

Sitting cross-legged in a tent playing a noisy game of Crazy Eights.

"You're cheating." I pointed at her.

"No, I'm not." She laughed, placing down the Jack of Spades. "You're just a sore loser."

I snickered and shook my head. "Cheater."

"Loser."

"Cheater!"

"Loser!"

Her eyes were dancing, brighter than they had that morning when we stood at the top of Yosemite Falls and looked at the stunning view. The green trees were vibrant against the gray rocks, the contrast breathtaking. Charlie had snapped a zillion photos, going on about how beautiful the national park was.

I just sat on a rock and watched her, love growing in my chest like an ever-expanding bubble.

And there she was sitting across from me, cheating at cards, and never looking more gorgeous.

Her laughter swam around me, blending with the music—"She Moves In Her Own Way." It was the perfect song for her. My best friend. Miss Unique. The girl I wanted to claim as mine. The girl I'd never had the courage to admit the truth to.

What if it screwed up our friendship?

What if we could never get back to our awesomeness?

She giggled, pressing her cards against her nose and wiggling her eyebrows at me.

"So cheating." I lurched forward, grabbing her wrist as she let out a delighted squawk.

She tried to wrestle free, but there was no way I was letting her go without checking her cards. She yelped and giggled, wriggling like a fish. I laughed and pushed her back onto the airbed on her side of the tent. She tried to roll away from me but I spun her onto her back, nestling myself between her legs so she couldn't move.

Snatching her other wrist, I held it above her head to ease her struggle, and then everything suddenly stopped moving.

The cards in her hand became the furthest thing from my mind.

All I could see were her hazel eyes.

They gazed up at me and I forgot how to breathe.

Her face was so close.

The wisp of her breath on my skin was fairy dust.

It worked a spell, broke the chains that had been holding me back.

Two years of pining came rushing into that one moment and I pressed my mouth to hers before I could stop myself.

Her lips were soft and pliable, her mouth tasting just as I imagined it—sweet like a peach.

It hit me then…what I was doing.

Kissing Charlie.

I was kissing my best friend.

I pulled back, aware of the line I'd just crossed.

My eyes must have been bugging out big time, and I couldn't read the expression on her face.

She just stared at me, shell-shocked. The cards dropped from her fingers.

I let go of her wrists, my heavy breathing making it impossible to apologize. I couldn't get the words out. I didn't know how to fix it.

But just as I started to lift myself off her, she grabbed my shirt and pulled me back down.

Her mouth was strong and determined, taking mine with a passion that gave away how much she wanted it.

I couldn't believe it.

She was into me.

That couldn't be possible. It made me hesitate until she opened her mouth and started frantically searching for my tongue. I met her halfway and we got caught in a pocket of heat and flavor.

Her tongue was the best thing I'd ever tasted.

Her body was the best thing I'd ever touched.

I had to feel it. Explore it. My hands moved without me even knowing. I delved into her riotous hair first, thick locks of beauty that I could wrap my fingers around. But then I wanted more.

My hand glided down her side, searching for an opening, a chance to touch her skin.

It was smooth perfection. The shape, the texture. I wanted to memorize every inch of it.

She shifted beneath me, weaving her arm around my shoulders and fisting my shirt. Her sweet moan ignited the fire I'd been trying to deny myself. It gave me the courage to try to unhook her bra. Turned out to be a bigger mission than I thought.

But then she laughed and helped me out.

Her eyes were diamonds as she slowly lifted her shirt and made herself vulnerable to me. I gazed at her breasts, tracing the shape with the pads of my fingers. With a nervous titter, she bit her bottom lip and I whispered the truth. "They're perfect. Not too big. Not too small." I grinned, palming her right breast and giving it a gentle squeeze. "The perfect fit for me."

A smile bloomed on her face. "Well, they're all yours."

It was an honor and I took it as such, guiding her back onto the mattress with the reverence she deserved.

A few minutes later, she was tugging the shirt off my body, and so began the wonders of exploration. We took it slow, marveling at the sensations we were both experiencing for the first time.

Inch by inch, we exposed more and more of ourselves to each other until there was nothing left to hide.

It was our awakening.

Time was stolen. Life outside was forgotten.

That tent became our palace and I lost myself…never to be truly found again.

TEN

CHARLIE

I shouldn't have said it.

Why'd I say it?

Cards?

That song?

"Dreaming Alone."

I never knew why I loved it so much until I stood in that motel room staring at Nixon and remembering how we lost our virginity together, in that tiny tent, in that amazing national park.

We spent ten days either hiking, dreaming or discovering the wonders of sex.

We didn't go all the way that first night. Nixon

had no protection, so instead we found different ways to reach climax. Talk about a heady rush. Nixon's fingers were supernatural, his tongue a freaking wand of pleasure.

I'd kissed every inch of his skin, watched his face as my touch brought him to orgasm. It'd been a thing of beauty.

The next morning, we'd crawled into the sunlight and made it our mission to find condoms. I thought I'd be nervous and scared about actually going all the way, but experiencing it together like that somehow eased the pressure. We were figuring it out, like two partners in crime, laughing through that first awkward encounter where he came within twenty seconds, and then slowly learning and building until waking up beside each other led to hours of passion, then dozing, then more passion. We'd break for food—candy bars, usually. I remember licking chocolate off his lips. My giggles got sucked away by his hot kisses, and then we'd be naked again and trying out another position.

When we weren't high on pleasure, we were hanging out—talking, dreaming, planning a future together.

Our excitement would lead to kisses and yes, more sex. It was a honeymoon of sorts, and I'd never experienced anything like it again.

I hadn't slept with another man since Nixon.

I'd kissed a few but as soon as things got hot and heavy, I'd pull away. The thought of another man touching me in those intimate places just put me off.

My body belonged to Nixon Holloway. I couldn't seem to give it to anyone else.

"Dreaming Alone" finished on a strong beat, jerking me out of my stupor.

I blinked and rubbed my forehead, struggling to breathe.

"You know, I just, um…realized I don't have any cards. So…"

Nixon looked down at the faded bedspread and nodded. "We should probably have an early night anyway. There's still a long way to go. I think I'll just read, then go to sleep."

I nodded. "Sure, yeah. I'll just, um…" I indicated to the bathroom with my thumb.

"I'll go find us some pizza." Keeping his eyes down, he quietly walked out of the room while I zombie shuffled to the shower.

Closing the bathroom door, I pressed my forehead against the wood, shutting my eyes against the burning tears.

"What a waste," I whispered. "It was such a waste."

I'd wanted him for months. It hadn't been love at first sight for me. But Nixon had grown on me faster than I expected. My serious crush started halfway through my junior year, and then came that awkward fear that I'd somehow screw things up if I let on.

So we kept playing a game of pretend, enjoying each other's company and growing more in love as the days ticked by.

We spent every waking minute we could together.

His parents didn't like me. I was a threat—unpredictable, too like Reagan for their fears to rest.

So we spent most of our free time hanging out at my place. My parents loved Nixon. Who wouldn't?

We'd listen to music, play games, read beside each other…whatever.

Just be.

We were really good at just being together.

"Why Don't You Love Me" filtered under the bathroom door.

I snickered and coughed out a cynical laugh. "Seriously?"

The music taunted me with another memory.

I used to lie on my bed, clutching a pillow to my chest and belting out those words, wishing Nixon would love me the way I loved him. Not even realizing that he did.

We'd wasted all of senior year.

And then that magical summer Nixon crossed a line…and it was perfect.

Until we got back to LA with our dreams firmly intact, only to have them torn to shreds by a father who knew I'd never be good enough for his son.

ELEVEN

NIXON

I didn't sleep well. I spent most of the night hyper-aware that Charlie was in the bed just feet from mine. I had to dodge memories of how her naked skin felt beneath my fingertips, how hot her mouth was. It was so easy to relive that sensation of her wrapped around me while I came inside her. Even after all this time it felt fresh and crystal clear.

We'd belonged to each other in every way we could.

But that was back then.

Four years on and I belonged to someone else.

I should have been thinking about my last time

with Shayna, but I couldn't remember it. Every time I started picturing her naked body or feeling her beneath me, she'd morph into Charlie.

I groaned, feeling like a dirty cheater.

The phone beside my pillow vibrated, then started ringing. I jerked out of my foggy slumber and scrambled to answer it.

"Hello," I croaked, rubbing my eyes and wondering what the time was.

"I miss you," Shayna whispered. "Where are you right now?"

I rubbed my forehead, grabbing my watch to check the time.

Shit. It was ten o'clock.

I glanced at Charlie's bed. She was still dead to the world, her hair a stormy blue sea on the pillow. My lips tugged into a smile before guilt reminded me that I was talking to my girlfriend. I swiveled back to face the window and whispered, "I'm still in Lexington, baby."

"You haven't left yet? I thought you were getting home as fast as you could."

I winced and raked a hand through my hair. "I slept really badly last night, and your call actually woke me."

"I thought you sounded groggy. You're not hung over, are you?"

"No," I snickered.

"What did you and Chuck do last night?"

"Nothing. I just went to bed early and read."

"Typical." She snickered. "You probably got so caught up in your book, you read until the early hours of the morning."

I hadn't actually, but I forced out a guilty chuckle. It wasn't like I could tell her the truth.

"Well, drive safe today, okay? I need you home. We've got a lot to talk about, and as soon as school goes back I know you'll be sucked into your studies again. You perfect A student, you." The pride in her voice was endearing, pulling my lips into a smile.

"I'll drive like the wind today, okay?"

"Don't break any laws, but yeah. Get home to me."

"I will."

"You better." She laughed. "Okay, I'm off to do my workout with the girls, and then we're going shopping after work." Her voice bounced around with excitement.

I raised my eyebrows, my stomach knotting.

Shopping with the girls.

It felt like a snippet into my future. My mind jumped forward to me in a suit, working long hours while Shayna went out and spent all the money, returning home with fistfuls of bags and thousands of dollars' worth of bills.

I squeezed my eyes shut and pinched the bridge of my nose.

"Love you, baby."

"Love you," I murmured and hung up, glancing over my shoulder when Charlie moaned and rolled over in bed.

Rubbing her eyes, she sat up and murmured, "What time is it?"

"Ten o'clock."

She glanced my way and gave me a sad smile before disappearing into the bathroom.

We hadn't really spoken much the night before. We quietly ate our pizza in front of *That 70s Show* reruns. I went to take a shower and when I got out, Charlie had her headphones on and was looking at pictures on her computer. I left her to it, read my book, then tried (and failed) to go to sleep.

So much for a last hurrah. All the road trip seemed to be doing was unearthing old, painful wounds that neither of us could talk about. How the hell did I come out and admit that deep down I knew I'd never been enough for her? I was too boring, and she'd quietly slipped out of my life to avoid having to admit it to my face.

That tent in Yosemite had been an out-of-world bubble, and when we returned to reality it must have hit her full in the face. Being trapped in a life with me was not going to work.

I'd spent hours locked in confusion, trying to figure out why she'd just gone.

Mom had been livid at Charlie for hurting me the way she did.

"I knew she was going to do something like this to you." She'd rubbed my back and tried to make me feel better. "You don't deserve this, Nixon. She's not worthy of you."

At first I tried to deny all her claims, but it was actually Dad's calm reasoning that helped me see the truth in the end.

"She was unstable and flighty. The way she left

is proof enough. Son, you probably don't want to hear this, but I think staying with you would have made her feel tied down. You're a rock-solid guy who deserves a woman who can appreciate you. It's better that she's left now rather than stringing you along only to wound you later. You have an amazing life ahead of you. Don't let that girl and what she did steal any more of it." Dad gave me a sad, heart-wrenching smile. "We have to protect each other. Don't let this beat you, son. You hold your head high and you fight for the future you deserve."

Dad probably thought his rousing speech had inspired me, but really it'd just helped me figure out that there was no point fighting when I didn't have anything to fight for.

I wasn't worthy of Charlie Watson. She needed some artistic guy who could drop everything at a moment's notice, be spontaneous and fun.

Her boyfriend was probably just like that. She said they were on-again/off-again, and that suited her.

She would have been a caged bird with me.

Still, I wish she'd had the guts to tell me. The way she left hurt like nothing I'd ever experienced before.

She stole a chunk of my heart the day she didn't show up…and I'd never recovered.

Worry was thick in my chest as I drove to Charlie's place.

I'd been calling her all day, but to no avail. She was

outright ignoring me and I didn't understand why.

We were supposed to meet up the night before but she texted me to say she had to bail. No explanation.

I tried to get into a conversation with her about it, but her only reply was: Tell you later.

The next day was later so I waited around, texting, calling, worrying.

Pulling up beside her little house, I glanced at her window. The curtains were drawn and I immediately jumped to the conclusion that she was sick.

I actually felt sorry for her as I ran up the path. I wanted to assure her that just because I'd seen her naked didn't mean I'd be grossed out if she was sick. Just because our relationship had shifted out of the friend zone didn't mean we couldn't still be best buds. I needed her to understand that. It was vital.

Knocking on the door, I'd already started formulating my speech when her mother appeared.

"Hey, Mia." I grinned. "Is Charlie okay?"

Mia's smile was sad and resigned. Her gaze darted to the floor. "She's not here, Nixon. She's…gone."

My forehead wrinkled. "Gone? What do you mean?"

"She's, uh…left. Moved to Montana for a while. Her father's driving her up there now."

I nearly fell off the front step. "What?"

"Montana. Her aunt lives there. Charlie's decided to go and stay with her for a while."

"Why?" I kind of barked the word, confusion making my head reel. "I don't understand. We had…plans."

"Well, you know Charlie. Everything's always last minute." Mia's voice was clipped, so unlike her.

I narrowed my eyes and she gave in with a sigh.

"She doesn't want to hurt you. But I think it's for the best." She gazed past my shoulder, her face flashing with what I thought was anger.

"Is Charlie mad at me?"

"No." Mia shook her head and finally looked my way, her eyes brimming with sympathy.

"What the hell is going on?" I whispered.

A tear trickled down Mia's cheek and she brushed it away before it could get very far. "I know she's your best friend and it must be very strange to have her disappear this way, but please trust that she's doing this for you. What you had this summer can't become reality."

My cheeks flamed as I wondered how much Charlie had given away.

I'd told my parents about my change of plans, but I'd mentioned nothing about the sex.

"Some things just aren't meant to be. Even though they feel right at the time, long term…" Mia's voice trailed off and for a second, I had to wonder if she even believed what she was saying. "You need to go live your life, Nixon. Be the man you were born to be."

It sounded like horseshit. The man I wanted to be was centered around Charlie. She was everything. She was the only one who ever made me feel like a man.

"I don't… I don't understand."

"I know." Another tear tracked down Mia's nose. She brushed it away and sniffed. "I wish I could explain it all. It's very unfair and confusing for you." Again, Mia's voice turned hard and kind of brittle before wobbling with tears. "But she made me promise. She needed to go, and she needs you not to track her down."

"Why? Why is she doing this?"

Mia's lips trembled, her chin bunching as more tears fell. "It's for the best. You two aren't going in the same direction, and it's better to end things now than break your hearts later."

"But—"

"Please, Nixon. I know it's hard, but you just have to accept what you don't understand. You and Charlie don't have a future together. Move on with your life."

Charlie popped out of the bathroom dressed in a pair of shiny blue pants and a Chaos tank top. Grabbing her orange and purple checkered hoodie, she threw it on, then pulled her hair free. It fell across her shoulders and breasts, framing her cherub face.

My breath was stolen for a second, even though I didn't want it to be.

She'd hurt me. I needed to feed off that, let it fuel me through the day. I had a girl at home who missed me, wanted me to hurry up and get to her side. Charlie left without even giving me the courtesy of a rebuttal, or a goodbye.

Grabbing my clothes, I headed for the bathroom. "We're running later than I wanted, so hurry up and get your stuff organized. We'll hit the road as soon as you're ready to go."

She nodded and got busy while I slipped into the bathroom and caught a glimpse of myself in the mirror. My large forehead was crinkled with worry lines, my dark brown eyes void of any spark. I felt like my gaze had been dead since she left me. Even Shayna couldn't make them sparkle the way

Charlie had.

My parents spent the rest of the summer convincing me it was for the best. Charlie was a high school friend, and high school was over. It was time to step up and become an adult. By the time I started UCLA a few weeks later, I was hungry for the classes, the readings, the study. I needed a distraction—anything to stop missing the girl who'd brought me to life.

Charlie was ready when I got out of the bathroom, so we packed up and grabbed a drive-through breakfast on our way out of town. I'd agreed to drive for the first half of the day and Charlie would take the second.

As I sipped my coffee, I kept stealing glances at her, even though I didn't want to. I should hate the girl beside me, but she made it so damn difficult.

Her head was bobbing like she was singing along to music, but there was no music playing. It was starting to grate on my nerves. She hadn't put on tunes like I expected, and the dead silence was a freaking killer.

Eventually I snapped, "What song is in your head right now?"

"Um…" She bit her lips together, her cute nose scrunching.

"Don't make something up, just sing the words. Go."

Her eyebrows rose. She obviously wasn't used to snappy Nixon, but she hadn't been around me over the last four years. My personality had slowly whittled away to turn me into the studious Nixon Holloway who liked nothing more than acing every class, studying on the weekends, and going out of my way to make my parents and Shayna proud. They were the people in my life who'd never let me down. It was my job to make them happy.

"Come on, Charlie. Sing."

She cleared her throat, then softly sang, "Hey, I was doing just fine…"

I held my breath, her voice like a sweet caress as she rattled off the first couple of lines before looking at me.

"Do you know it?"

"No." I shook my head, kind of annoyed that I didn't. When we'd compared playlists, I thought I still had my king status. At high school I knew more about music than she ever did. I was the music king.

But Shayna wasn't into it the way I'd been, and we just didn't listen to it all the time at home.

"It's called 'Closer.' It's by the Chainsmokers."

"Can I hear it?"

She cleared her throat and hesitated before pulling out her phone. She looked kind of reluctant as she scrolled through her music, and when the song started playing, I understood.

I didn't know why, but the music kept cursing us, bringing up songs that seemed to hit me right between the eyeballs.

I gritted my teeth as "Closer" filled all the spaces in the car, the lyrics bouncing off the windows and right back at me.

Out of the corner of my eye, I saw Charlie's lips purse, and then she spun to look out her window. For a second I wondered if she was crying. But then I told myself that couldn't be the case because she'd left me. She made the decision for both of us, because she obviously hadn't wanted the life we'd both dreamed up in that tent in Yosemite.

TWELVE

CHARLIE

Nixon was mad at me. He hadn't yelled or outright ignored me, but I could feel this vibe oozing out of him.

I hated it.

It took a lot to make Nixon mad, which was why we'd never fought in high school. In fact, we'd never really had an argument unless it was a slightly heated discussion about something to do with music or movies. Basically we'd agreed on everything and occasionally had to convince the other to win them over.

Other than that, our lives had been peaceful and

awesome.

"Nothing but awesome," I whispered.

"What was that?" Nixon glanced at me from the passenger seat. He'd been reading his Kindle since crossing into Arkansas.

I'd kept my mouth shut and done nothing more than hum along to the odd song. It'd been the longest frickin' day in the world. I was over it.

The trip back to LA was supposed to be a chance to make up for what we'd lost.

And I'd wasted a whole day lamenting the fact that I couldn't change the past.

This was possibly my last chance ever to make up for what I'd done, and I couldn't let this precious opportunity slip through my fingers. Time was running out. Once we reached LA, he was going to reunite with his girlfriend and before that happened, I needed him to know how much I still cared about him.

"Long Way Home" popped up on my screen and started pumping through the speakers. I looked at the only person I'd ever considered my true best friend and tried out some raw honesty.

"I miss our awesomeness. You made high school brilliant and wonderful. I miss it so much. I wish we could go back in time and just get stuck in this never-ending cycle."

"You want to relive junior and senior year over and over?" His voice was dry with sarcasm, his eyes still locked on the Kindle. A muscle in his jaw worked.

I shook my head and mumbled, "I know it

sounds dumb."

"Actually it doesn't." He scratched the side of his forehead. "I loved it too. It *was* awesome."

"I wanted our road trip to be the same." I swallowed.

Lowering his Kindle, he flashed me a sad smile. "You can't recreate the past, Charlie. What we had is gone."

I worked my jaw to the side, wondering if he was about to ask why. He had every right to. I was the reason it had all fallen apart and damn, he deserved a straight answer.

Noticing an exit up ahead, I pulled off the highway and followed a sign that said: Peyton—10 miles.

"What are you doing?" Nixon sat up in his seat.

"Let's stop for dinner. I've never heard of Peyton, but it's bound to have a diner or some place we can eat."

I'd tell him over dinner, let it all out in a rush if I had to.

My mind nearly short-circuited as I tried to formulate my spiel. I had to be careful not to destroy family ties, so my honesty had to be curbed, spoken in a tactful way that wouldn't ruin everything I'd tried to achieve by taking off.

My stomach twisted into a painful knot.

Man, did I seriously have the guts to go through with it?

Stop being such a coward!

But how do I say it?

Nixon, I wasn't good enough for you. I'm probably

still not, but hey, I'm selfish enough to forget all that and just be with you anyway. You're cool with me ruining your life, right?

I grimaced and gripped the wheel, keeping my eyes trained on the road ahead.

"Clark's Bar," Nixon finally murmured, pointing out his window as we entered the small town.

I leaned forward to spot the sign out the windshield, then started searching for a place to park. It wasn't hard to find one. The town seemed like a sleepy, peaceful place with basically all the traffic being local.

We headed for the bar and soon found ourselves in a warm, friendly place that had an Old West saloon-type feel—cozy brown and orange tones, a wooden floor, and a woman with wild blonde hair sitting on the stage strumming her guitar.

Her voice was smooth and easy to listen to.

I didn't recognize the song until Nixon snickered. "'This Town.' Good song."

He walked to one of the free tables near the bar and took a seat. I slowly followed him, absorbing the lyrics like they were written for me and Nix.

Yet another tune encouraging me to make it right, to fix what I had ruined years before.

Pulling out a wooden chair, I caught the guy behind the bar staring at me. He was tall and gorgeous—sandy hair tied back in a ponytail, broad shoulders, a serious smile. I raised my fingers to indicate two beers. He pointed at the taps and mouthed, "Bud Light?"

I gave him a thumbs-up and he got to pouring.

Pulling out some cash from my back pocket, I slapped it on the table, ready to hand it over when the drinks arrived.

"Ordered us some beers."

"Not for me." Nixon shook his head. "I still want to knock off a few more hours before we settle somewhere. I want to drive sober."

"Aw, come on, Nix. Have a beer, have some fries. Let's chillax for a bit."

His head whipped to face me, his glare kind of pointed. "I have to get home."

"Yeah, yeah, I know. You want to see your girlfriend." I didn't mean to snap the words; they just kind of popped out that way.

He pressed his lips together, obviously holding in whatever he had to say.

"I'm sorry," I whispered.

"For what?" He looked at me, his brown eyes trying to see right through me.

I opened my mouth, hoping the right words would magically pop out, but then the big guy arrived with our beers. Placing them down, he looked between us and then stuck out his hand to Nixon. "Josh. I own this place. Don't recognize either of you."

I smiled at his deep Southern drawl.

"We're just passing through." Nixon shook his hand.

"Heading for LA." I stuck out my hand. "Charlie, the hungry horse."

Josh gave me a half smile as he engulfed my tiny

hand in his. "Well, we do the best burgers in the state. You want to try our chef's special?"

"Mostly definitely." I grinned.

"Make that two." Nixon nodded at him before he walked away to put in our order.

I wrapped my fingers around my glass and gulped back the beer. It was cool and refreshing, just what I needed to find my courage.

Shuffling in my seat, I leaned my elbows on the table and tried to smile at Nixon. He wasn't looking at me, his gaze fixed on the singer as she brought the song to a finish.

Cheers went up around the bar, the loudest being from the big guy, Josh.

"Thank you, baby." The singer winked at him as she took the guitar off her lap, exposing a cute little baby bump. "I'm just taking myself a drink break, y'all. Don't go anywhere, now."

Her giggle was cute, enticing a few more whistles and a catcall to not take too long.

Josh hollered from behind the bar to leave her be while those around him laughed. The people in the place obviously knew each other well, and from the few odd glances Nix and I were getting, they weren't used to strangers…and didn't necessarily trust them either.

I smiled at the wrinkled-face guy beside me, then glanced at Blondie when she passed our table.

"You were great," I called to her.

She stopped and spun to face me. "Why, thank you. If you have any requests, y'all just let me know."

"Thanks." I nodded at her.

She rested her hand on the back of Nixon's chair. "I don't recognize you two. I'm Rachel."

"Nice to meet you." Nixon smiled at her. "We're just passing through."

Man, he was handsome when he put on that polite charm.

Thing was, it was genuine too.

Nixon was the nicest guy I'd ever met.

I averted my gaze from my heart's desire and studied the stage with its empty stool, microphone stand, and lonely black piano. I had to think of something to take the edge off the raw emotion scraping through me.

For most of my life my main goals had been happiness and fun. I'd never done well with conflict or negative emotion. That was probably why it'd been so easy to run to Montana. It would have been impossible to break up with Nixon if I'd seen his face. So I took the coward's way out. And my parents let me. They didn't want me caught up in some war that could only end in heartbreak. Indignation helped them pack my bags.

They didn't want me involved with a family that didn't think I was good enough. Mom and Dad had fought that their whole lives. They wanted better for me.

Problem was, better than Nixon didn't seem to exist.

"You play?" Rachel caught my attention with a soft nudge to my shoulder. "I see you staring up at that stage."

"Oh." I shook my head and forced a smile. "I was just wondering who played the piano."

"That'd be my Josh." She grinned, her face taking on that gooey quality of somebody in love. Gently caressing her baby bump, she looked to the bar and smiled at her man. "He always says he's too busy to play on nights like this, but truth is, my big grizzly bear just don't like playing in public. Such a shame too, because I'm sure these folks would love to hear him. Baby sure does."

My smile turned into a genuine grin. The affectionate look on her face was adorable.

"Baby likes the piano?" I pointed at her belly.

"I'm certain of it. I wish it was played more."

"Oh really?" I raised my eyebrows and tipped my head towards Nixon. "He plays."

His eyes bulged, then narrowed into a tight glare, worry skittering around the edges of his expression.

"Don't you do this to me, Charlie Watson."

I was pretty sure he was thinking something along those lines, and it made me giggle.

My lips rose into a wicked grin and my eyebrows started wiggling. I couldn't help it.

"Well, you should get on up there." Rachel patted his shoulder. "We'd love to hear ya."

"I haven't played in a really long time." Nixon was still glaring at me, but it was a losing battle. His lips were twitching. Maybe he could tell how much I wanted to hear him play again. How reliving just a snippet of those lunch hours in the music suite messing around on the instruments and making up stupid songs would mean the world to me.

Nixon had a great voice, and he could play. Our common ground had always been music. It connected us in this almost spiritual way, and if I could just snatch a moment of it…

"You know, if you get up there, I'll sing with you," Rachel encouraged him.

Nixon's face bunched with reluctance. "No, I shouldn't."

"I bet you're still really good," I singsonged.

Running his long fingers up the full beer glass, he forced out a chuckle. "If I have to get up there and play, you have to get up there and sing. There's no way I'm enduring the shame all by myself."

My lips pursed as I fought a smile. Not that I was overly keen on getting up there and embarrassing myself in front of a bunch of strangers, but I was suddenly desperate to hear Nix play.

So, slapping the table, I stood and pointed at the stage. "Lead the way, piano man."

THIRTEEN

NIXON

I was such a freaking idiot.

I should have known better than to goad Charlie into doing something stupid.

The girl had no shame. Of course she'd sing in order to dump me in it.

Every eye in the place landed on us as we climbed up onto the tiny stage. Rachel grabbed a spare mic and set it up next to the piano while I took a seat and started to sweat.

Rubbing my hands together, I lightly placed them on the keys, memories flooding back like a tidal wave—Charlie dancing around the music room, singing with abandon while I pounded the keys and harmonized with her.

My throat swelled as I tried to block them out.

I was still trying to figure out what her apology was for. Was it because she gave away a little jealousy when she talked about me getting back to my girlfriend?

Or was it something deeper?

She looked like she had something to say, her hazel eyes at war while she sat at the table staring at me.

Was she jealous? The thought was a lick of fire in the back of mind. I'd talked myself into believing that our Yosemite lovefest had been one-sided. Like I'd loved that tent utopia and she'd just put on a good show.

I could never make myself fully believe it though. I'd felt her fold in my arms. She'd given in to her desire with a passion that met mine strength for strength.

Being around her again made the memories so colorful and vibrant. Hanging out was the easiest thing in the world, like we'd only been apart for days not years.

I wanted to be mad at her for the rest of the trip home. Read my damn Kindle until I had no new books left.

Minimal contact. Keep things quiet and easy.

But she made that impossible.

Only Charlie Watson could somehow get me onto a stage like this.

Only Charlie Watson could keep me there with

her nervous, excited grin.

Rachel introduced us. "Charlie and Nixon, folks. The travelin' duo."

A few confused cheers went up, then dead silence.

Expectant silence.

I glanced at Charlie, who was staring down at me. Worry flickered over her features before she winced.

I laughed at her cute expression, then started drumming the top of the piano, giving her a steady beat for "We Are Young."

She picked it up without me having to say a thing and came in right on time.

It was a stinging reminder of how in sync we'd always been.

But it was also a thing of beauty.

I came in for the second part of the first verse, my fingers dancing on the keys like they could never forget, even if I wanted to.

Singing with Charlie had always sent a thrill right through my body. Goose bumps rippled over my skin while my chest expanded with a warm fuzz I hadn't felt in a really long time. I loved how we sounded together, and the smile on her face as she sang.

And I wasn't the only one.

By the second chorus, the entire bar was into it, bobbing their heads, pointing at us while they commented to their neighbor, smiling.

Rachel jumped up just before the bridge kicked in and started singing, "Carry me home…"

Charlie and I did backup vocals, and the three of us sounded freaking awesome because we were having a blast.

My best friend grinned at me while she sang her little solo. Then I leaned into the mic and came in, building up the song to the final chorus where she started waving her arms. She soon had a bunch of people doing the same.

As soon as I wrapped up the song, cheers erupted from the crowd.

Charlie laughed, the sound melodic and sweet. She took my hand and we bowed together.

My entire body was buzzing as we headed for our table, getting pats on the back and compliments along the way. When I sat down to take in the monster burger on my plate, I couldn't do anything but shoot Charlie a wide grin and raise my glass.

"What are we toasting?" She raised her beer.

"I don't know." I laughed and tapped my glass against hers before gulping down half the beer.

It felt damn good.

It made me realize how impossible it was to stay mad at Charlie.

And how impossible it was not to feel alive when I was around her.

FOURTEEN

CHARLIE

We ended up staying the night in Peyton.

We'd both had one too many beers to safely drive, so Rachel directed us to a nearby inn—the cutest little place. It was a shame we couldn't take our time. But Nixon's alarm went off when it was supposed to, rousing us both from Dead Land.

I groaned. "Shut that thing up, will ya?"

"I can't," he moaned. "We've got ground to make up today."

Flinging his covers back, he stood tall and stretched with a loud yawn. I peeked my eyes open and enjoyed the shape of his taut arm muscles.

He'd never be a super-strong stud or anything. He wasn't particularly muscly or sporty, but he was gorgeous to me. I loved his lean frame and the fact that I could wrap my arms all the way around him.

His curves and contours were sexy and beautiful. I could still picture his naked body in that hot little tent. Sweat glistened on his skin while I straddled him and traced a line from his collarbone to below his belly button. He'd gazed up at me with the kind of affection I'd never felt from anyone.

I was all that mattered.

Yosemite had been the happiest time of my life—Nixon's arms around me, his soft lips trailing kisses down my neck. I'd pictured an entire life of that.

But they were foolish dreams that hadn't considered the real consequences of everything we wanted. The reality check punched like thunder, shocked like lightning. My aunt spent months trying to coax a smile out of me. Not even Montana's breathtaking beauty could help me see past my pain.

The memories made me swallow and close my eyes. I'd allowed Nixon to have the life he was worthy of. I could never hate myself for that.

He had security, his family…and a girlfriend.

Clenching my teeth, I got up and dressed, then loaded up the car while Nixon had his turn in the bathroom. In spite of my sadness, I was determined the day would be fun like the night before. Nixon had been his old self again, laughing and having a good time. I needed to keep that going. We still had two days together…and a lot could happen in that time.

It was almost seven o'clock when we hit the road. I figured we'd knock off a couple of hours before breakfast. I gulped down some water from my bottle as we drove out of Peyton. Nixon was still kind of groggy but his lips tugged into a smile as he waved goodbye to Clark's Bar.

I'd never forget that night—Rachel with her baby bump, Josh and the dreamy way he watched her on stage, getting the entire bar to raise their hands and sing "We Are Young" with us.

"Pure epicness," I murmured.

"What was that?"

I smiled. "Last night was epic. I had so much fun. Thanks for getting up on stage with me."

His laughter had that morning croak to it—husky and sexy. "The things I let you drag me into."

"Aw, come on, you had fun, didn't you?"

"I was with you. Of course I had fun." He winked and then started singing the chorus of "Good Time."

I giggled and passed him my phone. I didn't have to ask him to look up the song; he knew what I was doing and searched for the upbeat tune on Spotify. Thirty seconds later, my phone was plugged into the stereo system and we were rocking out to "Good Time," singing the parts the way we always used to.

It was a snapshot of our past and it set the perfect tone for our day of driving.

The hours flew by. We sang, laughed, reminisced about high school, then chatted about mundane stuff turned interesting because I was talking to Nixon.

We knocked off two hours before stopping for a quick breakfast, then managed another six before stopping for a late lunch. We wanted to reach Albuquerque by the end of the day, which meant we still had another five hours to go. We probably wouldn't get there until after nine, but Nixon had called ahead and booked us a room at a hotel near the highway.

He held the door open for me as we stepped into Big Bear Diner. It looked like a family-owned business—wooden interior, checkered tablecloths, huge meals and friendly smiles. Decent music pumped through the sound system, loud enough to be heard but quiet enough not to disrupt conversation. I instantly loved the place.

"Smell that?" I sniffed.

"Oh yeah." Nixon wiggled his eyebrows. "So good."

I laughed as he followed me to a big, round booth in the corner. The place was half full and the smell of bacon was rich in the air.

"I know it's lunchtime, but I'm totally getting the big breakfast." Nixon opened his menu the second we sat down on the squishy red leather seat.

My nose wrinkled as I browsed the glossy

pages, but it didn't take me long to settle on a club sandwich and steak fries. It was just the ticket. I also ordered a glass of Sprite. I needed the sugar kick to keep me going.

"Can't believe you still drink soda." Nixon snickered.

My head jerked to look at him. "And you don't?"

"Nah. Too full of sugar." He shrugged.

"In other words, your girlfriend won't let you drink it anymore."

His embarrassed smile and the way he raked his fingers through his hair told me I was right. His brown locks kind of flopped over his forehead, the lack of hair product giving it a soft, messy look. I liked it. It was way more relaxed than that slicked-back do. I bet it was his human resources office girl's idea to make him look that snazzy, dress that fancy…and eat all healthy.

"Is she one of those size four health freaks who only eats rabbit food and exercises for like five hours a day?"

He laced his fingers together and rested them on the table, forcing a tight smile. "No, but she does like to eat healthy. And she only makes me eat that way too because she cares about me."

He bit his lips together.

"She's a control freak, isn't she?"

He stared at his phone, then started spinning it on the table as he tried to deny my statement. "She… I like being looked after. It's—"

And then his phone started ringing.

Picking it up, he saw the caller and clenched his jaw before mumbling, "I have to take this."

He shuffled out of the booth and walked away so I couldn't hear the conversation.

I could tell he was talking to her though…or his mother.

The look was the same.

Whoever he was talking to was ragging on him—demanding, pressuring…and he was saying all the right things because he was an expert in pleasing people.

The heavy stone in my belly rattled beneath the pent-up guilt I didn't want to face. I'd left because I thought it was best for him, but as I sat there watching his tight expression, I had to wonder if I'd made the biggest mistake of our lives. Had I sentenced him to a life he never even wanted because I was too scared that we'd lose the fight?

I didn't want to be the nuclear bomb that blew his family apart, knowing what they'd already lost. His father had been so damn convincing.

And Nixon had never followed me or tried to track me down. I never expected him to, but I'd still lain awake for hours murmuring wishes into the darkness, hoping he'd show up on Aunt Jessica's doorstep.

He never did.

He got over me and moved on, scoring himself a girlfriend who was nothing like me.

I blinked and looked out the window while Nixon finished his phone call.

He returned to the table with a little sigh, then

flashed me a forced smile. As much as I wanted to avoid serious conversation, I had to break my own rule and say something.

The day was supposed to be nothing but light banter and fun, but I couldn't hold it in as his butt shuffled on the spongy seat and the muscle in his jaw worked big time. Clench, unclench, clench, unclench.

Sexy. So damn sexy.

I'm still in love with you.

That's what I wanted to say.

But I didn't. I went for a more subtle approach. "Are you happy?"

"What?" He frowned, his eyes still drilled on the table.

I nudged his elbow with my knuckles. "With your life. Are you happy?"

"Of course I am," he mumbled.

"So, you want to go to Columbia, and be with this girl. What's her name?"

"Shayna," he whispered.

"Shayna." I nodded. "Nice name." Trying to keep my voice upbeat was damn hard. The word was ash in my mouth, dark and acidic. "So, she makes you happy? You're happy with your life?"

"I just said I was! Why do you keep asking?" His eyes flashed to mine and then back down to the table. He started spinning his phone again and I licked my lips, heartsick at the fact that he was lying.

"I'd hate it if you were forced into a life you didn't want. It's really important that you follow your heart, and your dreams."

His laughter was brittle as he shook his head. Scrubbing a hand down his face, he pinched his nose, obviously fighting something. I was desperate to know what he really wanted to say, but in the end he just grumbled out more bullshit.

"Life doesn't work like that, Charlie. Not everyone's dreams come true. There needs to be a certain amount of sense thrown into the equation. There are other people to think about, and it's selfish to just blindly pursue what you want without considering anyone else."

The bitterness in his tone and the dark look on his face made it clear that he was thinking I'd left him for purely selfish reasons. The thought was brutal, but what did I honestly expect? In his eyes, that was exactly what I'd done.

If only I could tell him the truth. I wanted to unleash it all, but it'd just do more damage than good. It'd turn my last four years of torture into a complete waste.

Gritting my teeth, I took in a breath and finally managed, "Not all dreams are selfish."

"Your passion for photography took you to Montana. You quit on a college education to pursue a dream with no guarantees!"

"I quit on college so I could live a life that made me happy. I want to photograph every color that exists on this planet. I want to capture every face and every smile. And I want to see it all through my camera lens. A college classroom wasn't letting me do that."

Nixon's fingers shook as he rubbed his forehead. "Life can't be about having fun all the time. At some point you have to grow up and live a normal life."

"What's normal?" I bit back. "Two-point-four kids and a house? That's all well and good if you want that, but that can't be my normal. My normal can't be this strict, rigid set of rules and expectations. I want to travel, and see the world. I don't want to be tied down, and I don't need to be like everybody else to feel happy."

His gaze hit mine. The look in his eyes was heart-wrenching. Those sad brown eyes. If only he could understand how badly I wanted my dreams to include him. I'd just spouted off the plans we'd come up with in that tent. Traveling, exploring, adventuring together.

But then I'd gone and left him out of the equation.

And he'd moved on like he was supposed to.

I'd convinced myself it would make him happy. He'd be better off.

But…

Oh shit. What have I done?

FIFTEEN

NIXON

I wanted to shut her up with intelligent rhetoric. Put her in her place with excuses about how striving for constant happiness would only lead to a restless heart. But all I could do was sit there and stare at her.

I am going to make the worst fucking lawyer in the world.

I hated myself in that moment.

She deserved to be lashed with the truth. I wanted her to hurt for how much she'd hurt me. But I couldn't.

Because she was Charlie, and I'd always love

her.

The thought of hurting her made me sick, which was why I'd forced myself to let her go. I couldn't make her happy. What we'd had in Yosemite was just a dream.

The song ran through the back of my mind. I'd listened to it over and over when she first left. "Just a Dream" lamented with me, carried me through the end of that dark summer and into the life my parents wanted for me.

When I'd first told them about changing my plans and delaying college by a couple of years so Charlie and I could travel, they hadn't taken it well. But I'd been prepared to fight. It was Charlie, not just some chick.

They told me to think twice about it. Galivanting off on a world adventure and simply living in the moment was reckless. What about my future? A college education? A career?

They implied that Charlie was too wild and unpredictable, that she'd let me down.

I saw the fear in their eyes. They thought Charlie was too much like Reagan, that she'd take me free-climbing and I'd fall to my death.

But they didn't know her.

I tried to argue that she'd never do something like that to me. We were in love. She wasn't going to hurt me or break my heart.

But then she did.

I hated that they were right, because I was so convinced they weren't.

She was my best friend, and had become my

lover. The chemistry between us was smoking hot, built on a foundation of trust and friendship. What Charlie and I had was rock-solid.

Until she smashed it to pieces without so much as an explanation.

As I stared at her across the diner table, I wanted to cry, scream, yell…do something to unleash what I'd been holding back for the last four years.

My stomach was raw with nausea and I had to smash my teeth together in order to keep it in.

Charlie's face crumpled with regret. It was blatant; I wasn't reading her wrong. But it only confused me.

What the hell was she regretting?

She'd gone off and made all her dreams come true.

Well, most of them. She still had the travel thing on her agenda, but if anyone was going to make it happen, it'd be her. She didn't let life get in the way. She never had.

Wiping her finger under her nose, she gave me a pained smile while we both sat there holding it all in.

Damn, I wanted to know what was going through that brain of hers. She'd always been so open and honest with me. But that was four years ago, when we were the closest any two people could get.

I wanted to hear her admit she'd made a mistake. That she never should have left me.

But what would be the point?

I was with Shayna.

And Charlie didn't want me. If she did, she wouldn't have taken off like that.

She probably thought she was sparing my feelings somehow, and I needed to tell her she hadn't. What she'd done was brutal.

"I…" Charlie's mouth opened and closed for a second.

She'd always been allergic to conflict. Whenever someone was angry or sad, she'd go out of her way to make them smile, shift the tone to something fun.

Well, it wouldn't work this time.

Nothing she could say or do would make this better.

She'd hurt me. She'd stolen my dreams and set me on this path.

This restless path that I so desperately wanted to love but couldn't quite get there. This path that gave me the security I needed.

I had to keep reminding myself of that. Shayna was a good woman who'd never let me down.

Charlie was the exact opposite of that.

Looking away from her, I stared at my phone and started spinning it again. What the fuck else was I supposed to do?

"Live Life Loud" came on the radio and a movement from the corner of my eye caught my attention.

I glanced at Charlie. She was mouthing the lyrics and getting into the song. As soon as she saw me watching her, she started banging her head and rocking out on her air guitar. Blue hair splashed around her face, her exaggerated expressions tugging at me, forcing me to grin when I didn't want to.

Entertaining me wasn't going to solve the problem, and it pissed me off that I couldn't resist her.

I wanted to be mad at this girl, but she made it impossible.

She was rocking out to a song that epitomized who she was. Charlie lived life loud; she made the most of everything and she'd chased her dreams to become a photographer.

What the hell was I becoming?

A lawyer.

I'd wear gray suits to work and have to shine my shoes on the weekends. I'd drive some boring car and live in some boring house in a boring suburb.

The secure, safe life my parents wanted for me. Quiet and unassuming.

The exact opposite of the kind of life Charlie Watson would lead.

SIXTEEN

CHARLIE

My head-banging made him smile, but then our meal arrived and I had to stop dancing…had to invite back the big awkward I was trying to avoid.

How did I tell him?

How did I face it all and tell myself that what I thought was an act of pure selflessness had ended up doing more damage than good?

As I nibbled on my fries, memories from that night came flooding back with choking clarity.

I should never have answered the door. I'd been getting ready to go out and meet up with Nixon. I thought he'd shown up to surprise me rather than meeting up like we'd planned.

So I opened the door.

I stupidly swung back the wood, oblivious to the fact that my life was about to be ruined.

"Mr.... Mr. Holloway." I glanced past him to see if Nixon was waiting in the wings. No such luck. It was just me and him—the scary-ass lawyer.

"Hello, Charlotte."

Shit. He used my actual name. It was a really bad sign.

Gripping the door, I forced a polite smile and replied in a tiny voice, "Hello."

Smoothing a hand over his salt-and-pepper hair, he drilled me with the kind of look a prosecutor gives a guilty guy on the stand.

I swallowed, trying not to be thrown by it.

"I hope you don't mind me popping over unannounced like this, but I need to talk with you."

"Okay, um..." I scratched the side of my neck. My parents weren't home, so I wasn't about to invite him in. Not with that look on his face.

"It won't take long. But it's very important that I make myself clear."

"Clear?" My nose wrinkled. "On...what?"

His chuckle was soft but metallic, his smile hard. "Nixon told me what you two have planned. He's very excited, already making lists of everything you need to do in order to prepare."

I grinned. "That's Nixon for ya."

Mr. Holloway's mouth flatlined. "He's not going."

"Excuse me?"

"If you think you're going to pull our only living child away from us, you've got another thing coming."

Shock stole my voice for a second. "I'm not… I'm not pulling him away. We—"

"Traveling for a couple years before you even attempt college? Are you insane?"

His snap made me flinch. I gripped the edge of the door and tried not to sound intimidated. "It's not like he doesn't plan to go at all. We're just exploring for like a year."

"Which will turn into two, which will turn into three and before you know it, you're broke with no security. You don't stay young forever, Miss Watson. And I don't appreciate you filling my son's mind with this trash."

"It's not trash. We have a plan, and I would never do anything to lead him astray."

"Yes, yes, you say that now. But you're eighteen. You two don't know anything about life."

My nostrils flared. "I think you're being a little unfair. We may be young but we're not stupid."

"Your plan is stupid. I tried to tell Nixon that but he wouldn't believe me. He's too caught up in his excitement to listen to reason. So I'm appealing to you."

I swallowed and tried to sound braver than I felt. "Sir, I don't know what you want me to tell you. But Nixon and I…well, we're together now, and we are very excited for our future."

Pinching the bridge of his nose, I got the distinct impression I was pissing him off. Shit, I was already scared enough of the guy; I didn't want to poke a raging bull. But come on, he was acting like a total dick.

"How do I explain this so that you'll understand?"

He sighed. "I will not allow you to destroy my son's life. You will not steal him from us this way."

I shot him an incredulous look. "I'm not stealing anyone. He loves you guys. He'll always be your son, no matter where he is in the world."

"My wife will not survive this. If you take him from us, it will be like reliving Reagan's death all over again."

"That is so unfair to Nixon," I whispered, then found the strength in my voice again. "Do you hear yourself right now? You can't put that kind of pressure on him."

"I want my son to have a wonderful life."

"And he will."

"With you?"

It was kind of impossible not to be insulted by the sharp sting in his tone. "I…I'll do everything in my power to make him happy."

"How can you say that? The only reason Nixon wants to travel right now is because of you. If you weren't in the equation, he'd be getting excited about college. As it should be. He's too intelligent for this, and his talent will be wasted if he goes off traveling. And if you think a cent of my money is going to help you take this reckless trip, then you can think again. I will cut off Nixon's financial supply if he chooses to use that money for anything other than college."

My frown deepened. We'd totally planned on using that money.

But I wouldn't let it deter me.

"Okay, fine." I threw up my hand. "We won't travel yet. He can go to college and I'll work my ass off saving for our trip. We can go after he's graduated."

Mr. Holloway's smile was hard and unrelenting.

"He'll need to think about entering the workforce then."

My eyes started to prickle as it hit me that no matter what I said, Nixon's dad would have a perfect rebuttal.

"Think about it. You'll be slaving away while he studies and figures out what he wants to do with his life. You'll go insane with boredom and restlessness, unwittingly putting pressure on him. You know how desperate he is to please the people he loves. He'd do anything for you, and you say you'd do anything to keep him happy, but be realistic. You're wild and spontaneous. He's the exact opposite. You're not a good match. You don't fit into the world he belongs in."

"But I love him," I squeaked.

"Then break up with him before any more damage can be done. I know it will hurt you both, but you'll move on and it'll be for the best. Do you really want to create a wedge in the family? We've already lost so much."

I scoffed and shook my head. "You're the one trying to create the wedge. If you'd just accept me and allow Nixon to follow his dreams—"

"He doesn't even know what his dreams are. He's following you. He hasn't even had a chance to work out who he is yet. You need to allow him to do that."

"But…why? I mean, how can you ask me to hurt him this way? Don't you want your son to be happy?"

"And you think you can make him that?" Mr. Holloway's expression and tone mocked me. "I'm his father. I know what's best for my own child, and I won't lose him to someone who's not even worthy of him."

Ouch. It stung like a slap to the face, and my expression must have told him as much.

With a sigh, he softened his voice. "Please hear my logic. I'm protecting you both from romantic notions that will only end in disaster."

"Or be brilliant," I retorted.

"The fact that you can't say that without your voice shaking tells me you understand what I'm trying to say. I know you don't want to hear any of this, but please, think about it. We will not support Nixon if he chooses to take this path with you. And right now he's too high on love to see anything clearly. It's up to you to save him. Think about who you are. Imagine the future. And do the right thing." His voice was so certain, it was hard not to buy in to what he was saying, but then he sealed it with a threat that made my skin prickle. "I'm not above using any resources or connections I have to protect my family. I know a lot of important people in this city."

I frowned, trying to figure out what the hell he was saying.

"Do you have any idea who I am and what I'm capable of?"

"You're...a lawyer."

He chuckled. "And you know what lawyers do, right? We make up stories for a living. We take tiny threads, little pieces of information, and weave them into believable stories. We convince judges and jurists of an individual's innocence or guilt. We have the power to save or destroy people. Tell me, what position do you think I'd take if I had to save or destroy you?"

"But I haven't done anything wrong!"

"It doesn't matter. I just have to convince people you have. And trust me. I am very, very good at what I do. It'll take me a two-minute phone call to bring a

restraining order against the girl who is stalking my son and threatening to destroy my wife's life. I can have articles published in magazines, papers…online. Social media is a powerful weapon, and people will believe anything. I could black mark you for the rest of your life. Think of the impact that will have on all the people you care about. Your mom with her little craft shop. I wonder how it would affect her business? And your dad, the dedicated school teacher. It'd make his job pretty tough when rumors about his psychotic daughter start circulating."

My lips parted in surprise, dread and fear swirling inside me like a toxic cocktail. The look on his face warned me to believe him.

"If you don't take this conversation seriously, you'll force my hand. I will not have you anywhere near my home…or my son."

"But…" My argument kind of died inside of me then. I wasn't capable of taking on a ferocious giant like Malcolm Holloway.

"Don't make him choose between us. Our family has been through enough. I need to protect the people I love."

"I'm not going to hurt him or destroy his life! That's what you're *trying to do right now!"*

He scoffed and shook his head. "You're too young to understand these things. Just trust me. You and Nixon don't have a future together."

"I'm not Reagan," I spat.

His eyes shot to mine, dark with thunderous warning.

I shrank away from his black look.

"Do the right thing." His voice shook. "You save our

family from falling apart and make the choice for him!" He pointed at me.

Tears burned my eyes as I gazed at the man's steely expression. "You're not going to fold, are you?"

"I don't fold. I win."

My nostrils flared as a spike of hatred shot through me. "You know it's not my choice. You're forcing me into a corner."

He nodded, turning away as if embarrassed by my tears.

"I can't break up with him." I shook my head. "There's no way I can look at his face and actually say the words."

Mr. Holloway nodded. "I understand. I can pass on a message if you need me to."

My heart sank. "Will he actually get it? Or will it just be whatever lies you choose to feed him?"

He sidestepped my question with a sad smile. "Think about our family and everything we've lost. Think about your family and everything you'll be saving them from. How do you think your parents will feel if their daughter has a restraining order placed against her? Nasty articles published about you? The right words told to the right people can really destroy someone's life."

"I should tell Nix what you're doing," I seethed.

"But you won't." His expression was hard yet confident. "Because you love him, and you know you'll only end up destroying his *life if you don't walk away."*

My throat swelled, making it impossible to argue back. What could I honestly say? To Mr. Holloway, I had no more worth than a dried-up piece of gum on the bottom of his shiny shoes.

"Do the right thing, Charlotte. Find a way to save us all a huge amount of pain."

He left a short while later and I stumbled to the couch. Mom and Dad found me in tears about twenty minutes later. I blubbered out the whole story, thinking they'd march me over to the Holloway's and demand that they stop acting like dicks. But instead they got angry, insisting I never go there again if they were going to treat me so badly.

They didn't want me with Nixon if his parents were only going to make it hard for us to be together. I argued that I loved him and we could fight the odds. But when I wiped the tears from my eyes and looked into their faces, I saw the truth.

They didn't think Nixon was right for me either…and they didn't want me ending up dating a guy whose parents wouldn't appreciate me.

Mom had spent most of her life putting up with judgments from her family, and my dad barely spoke to his in-laws.

The awkward wedge had caused so much heartache…so many tears.

I didn't want that for Nixon. His parents might be a little up themselves, but they were his parents and I couldn't tear them apart. Not after they'd lost Reagan.

And I couldn't rob Nixon of a college education or taint him with any black marks flung against me.

Mr. Holloway was right. Nix was too smart and talented to throw his life away on me.

So I did the only thing I could. I disappeared to Montana. If I saw Nixon, I would have folded like a deck of cards. So I took off in the night, stole away like a coward, desperately trying to convince myself I was doing the right thing.

I went for the clean break. Ignored all his calls and texts. Shut down my social media accounts. Went off the grid in the hopes it'd be easier.

It wasn't.

I dreamed about him every night. Missed him every day.

Aunt Jessica was kind and sympathetic. She rubbed my back as my stomach jerked with sobs. She distracted me with photography and helped me find some new dreams.

But they were never as bright and shiny as the ones Nixon and I had dreamed up in that tent.

Maybe that was why I'd never had the courage to actually leave and travel the world on my own.

Maybe all that time, I'd been waiting for him.

SEVENTEEN

NIXON

Well, lunch was a bust.

I offered to drive the rest of the way to Albuquerque, and it was a damn quiet ride.

Music was playing the whole time but there was no more head-banging, singing, laughter—any of the things that defined Charlie and me.

It was so weird being with her and not having fun.

I hated it.

But I wasn't funny or quirky enough to break the spell.

That was Charlie's job. I was just a backup

performer—never really good enough for her. When I told Mom that, she argued that Charlie wasn't good enough for me. She was horrified and disappointed that my best friend had taken off without so much as a goodbye. The look on her face told me she knew it would happen eventually. She was livid at Charlie for hurting me, and begged me not to find her. The words were like acid in my ears, but I eventually bought into them. College began and took over my life.

They'd always warned me that Charlie's impulsive nature would get me in trouble one day. And it kind of did. She made me buy into a dream that would never come to fruition. She'd always been such an idealist and, in spite of my practical nature, I truly believed we could make it happen. I thought the two of us were the perfect pair.

*****

By the time we reached the hotel, I was ready to combust. We unloaded the car and checked in, barely looking at each other. As soon as we reached the room, Charlie locked herself behind the bathroom door.

I dumped my bag at the end of my bed and raked a hand through my hair.

All I wanted was to get home to Shayna and be 'normal' again.

Except, the thing was…

I didn't want that.

I wanted the tent in Yosemite. I wanted my

senior year of high school.

I wanted those bursts of color I'd experienced since meeting Charlie in New York to last longer.

That was the normal I wanted again.

The normal I could never have.

The toilet flushed in the bathroom and I gritted my teeth, already dreading the evening. Thankfully it was late and I could use the excuse of another big driving day.

Our last one.

Shit. I wanted it to be good. No more of this tense silence!

I snatched the pillow off my bed and hurled it across the room just as Charlie opened the door.

Although unintended, my timing was perfect.

The pillow hit Charlie square in the face and she let out this surprised scream.

It was the funniest sound I'd heard all day and I cracked up laughing before I could stop myself.

"What are you, like eight?" She was trying to be mad but she ended up laughing the words as she picked up the pillow and threw it back at me.

I caught it and kept the game going.

Maybe it was the release I needed. Or maybe it was a chance to laugh with Charlie again.

She countered my next attack and leaped for her own ammunition. Snatching pillows, she let out this deep chuckle. The one I'd always adored.

"I am armed and dangerous now, Holloway."

"Bring it on, Watson."

With a yell she jumped onto her bed and took the higher ground, firing two pillows at me and batting away my attacks.

Snatching her pillows, I did a spin and launched them at her, getting knocked in the head by one of her pillow grenades. I laughed and raised my arm against her next pillow missile while inching closer.

She screamed when I grabbed her leg and gave it a tug. As she fell she snatched my shirt, dragging me down as well. There was no way she'd fall alone. Not when it came to a tussle.

I lurched forward with a laugh and then an oomph when I landed on her, then quickly lost my balance. Instinct kicked in and I grappled for something to stop my fall, but all I ended up doing was yanking the duvet and we flopped onto the floor together, Charlie's cheek cracking against mine.

"Ow," she groaned, rubbing her face.

"Sorry." I laughed, gently moving her hand to get a look. Her cheek was a little red, but nothing major. My own burned but my body was quickly turning numb as it registered the fact that Charlie was lying on top of me.

I should have been sliding away, walking away…any kind of *away,* really, but I couldn't move.

Because she was right there.

Her hazel eyes danced with laughter. Her perfect lips were inches from mine.

My fingers had to touch her. They slid across her soft cheek, remembering exactly what it felt like to hold her. I traced the curve of her ear and ran my fingers into her locks of vibrant hair. As soon as my hand cupped the back of her head, she dove for my mouth.

The urgency of her kiss told me so much.

It was all so familiar. The taste of her tongue, the way her body melded against mine. She bent her knees and ground into me, her breasts squishing against my chest. I groaned and cupped her tight butt, squeezing it and being transported back in time.

My body begged me to explore some more and before I could stop them, my fingers were wriggling beneath her shirt, finding silky soft skin, curves and perfect breasts.

She moaned into my mouth when I brushed my thumb across her erect nipple.

My dick danced with joy, growing hard and eager as her tongue twirled around mine.

I wanted to peel her clothes off, kiss and suck every inch of her.

Charlie in my arms was right.

It was natural.

It would have been so easy to trigger all her sweet spots again. Her panting breaths would grow fast and erratic as I brought her to orgasm, and then she'd scream out, making me feel like a frickin' superhero. Then she'd return the favor, sending me on a course around the sun before we'd finish together. Me buried inside her and riding that cloud that even after four years seemed so close, so touchable.

So incredibly unacceptable.

An image of Shayna shot through the back of

my brain. Me having to tell her—breaking her heart. A woman who'd only ever been good to me.

It wasn't fair. It wasn't right.

I was about to cheat on her with a girl who'd torn my heart to shreds.

The thought pulled me away with a fast jerk. I pushed Charlie off me and scrambled to my feet. Heavy breaths punched out of my chest as I tugged my sweater down to hide my erection. It didn't really work, so I turned my back on Charlie and stared bug-eyed at the wall.

"I'm sorry," she whispered. "I shouldn't have—"

"It wasn't your fault," I muttered, pissed off that...

I couldn't have her.

My shoulders slumped.

That was it. Right there.

She took off and started this whole fucking thing.

I was where I was because she turned her back on something amazing.

And I couldn't have her because I'd moved on like I was told to.

The good boy.

"Always the good boy," I seethed.

"What?"

"I'm a good boy." I scoffed and turned to look at her.

She stood, straightening her shirt with shaking hands. "You don't always have to be."

The tiny smile on her lips and the fire in her eyes

was all the permission I needed.

I closed the space between us in record time, grabbing her face and finally taking something *I* wanted. For me. Something for me.

EIGHTEEN

CHARLIE

His tongue was hot and fiery as it entered my mouth, reminding me of everything I'd been missing. I was way past horny as Nixon dipped his head and deepened the kiss.

I wanted to tear the clothes off his body. Lick his torso, go down on him, hear him moan with pleasure before letting him take me on the bed. Hard and fast would suit me fine. We could do slow and easy later in the night when our hearts had found their regular rhythms again.

Then in the morning we could…

The morning.

The next day.

Driving to LA.

Nixon's girlfriend.

Reality.

The words grew louder and louder, screaming over the chaotic passion trying to drive me forward.

Nixon cupped my breast, giving it a gentle squeezing and turning me on while his tongue skimmed my neck.

His touch tried to claim me, pull me back into dreamland, but then came the shouting again.

It wasn't right.

Sleeping with Nixon wouldn't be right.

So far, our love had only ever been pure. Pure passion. Pure innocence. Pure beauty.

If we did it in this hotel room, it'd change all that.

It'd turn Nixon into a cheater and me into the other woman.

"Stop," I whispered.

It was an effort. I wanted him to keep going so badly.

I even contradicted my words by fisting his hair and holding him against me for a second.

Squeezing my eyes shut, I grimaced and cried out, "Stop! We have to stop!"

Nixon jumped away from me, his face awash with pain. "I don't want to stop."

Neither do I!

I wanted to scream the words and then rush back into his arms, but I swallowed hard and croaked out what I was supposed to. "I won't turn you into a cheater."

"But I want you." His voice was broken and bruised. I nearly caved on the spot.

Pulling in a ragged breath, I pinched my nose and turned away from him. "You have a girlfriend."

His silence made tears swarm onto my lashes. And then he whispered, "I know."

"You can't cheat on her. You'll feel like scum, and it'd ruin everything between us."

"I know." He sighed.

Wrapping my arms around myself, I grabbed my shirt and squeezed. He wanted me.

I glanced over my shoulder and caught his eye.

He gave me a sad, pained smile.

It was tempting to shout at him for moving on when I couldn't.

If he'd just waited for me we could give in to the moment.

But I'd left him. I'd given him every reason to fall for another girl.

"I—"

"I can't stay in this room with you and not have you," Nixon whispered. "I won't be able to control myself."

His words made me smile. It'd be so easy to give in and write it off as a walk down memory lane. No harm. No foul.

But it wouldn't work.

Nixon would be ravaged by guilt, and if we did ever get back together, it would taint our whole relationship.

If there was one thing I never wanted to fuck up again, it was Nixon and me.

My lips rose into a shaky smile. "Let's just keep driving, then. The sooner we get home the sooner we can…figure this out."

He knew what I was saying, and the small spark in his eyes gave me hope.

There was still so much to say and do, but it looked like my second chance with Nixon could be just around the corner.

*****

We drove in agitated silence at first. We were both exhausted, but we kept pushing. LA was waiting for us. An old life. A new start.

I could almost taste it.

I drifted into a dreamy doze until the early hours of the morning when Nixon woke me to take over for him. He fell asleep as soon as we took off and didn't rouse until midmorning. By then I was ready to stop for coffee.

We were about two hours out from LA. As tempting as it was to just keep driving, I forced us to stop for a late breakfast in Newberry. We shared a massive stack of pancakes and got extra coffee to go.

Nixon took the last leg and I got music going as soon as I could.

"Another You" by Against the Current started us off and I bobbed my head to the beat. As much as the lyrics wanted to take me out, they couldn't. Because all I could do was look at Nixon and smile.

Hopefully my kisses last night had shown him how much I had never wanted to say goodbye in the first place. How being back together with him was everything I'd been craving.

When we reached the outskirts of LA, we both kind of tensed. Exhaustion and coffee were making me jumpy, and I figured Nixon wasn't looking forward to the next part of his life.

Breaking up always sucked. Would he have it in him to do it?

I totally understood the pain of hurting somebody and I wouldn't rush him, but man, I was desperate.

The sooner he was single, the sooner we could be together.

"This exit," I murmured when we neared the off-ramp.

He followed my directions and eventually pulled up beside the plaster-clad apartment I called home.

"This looks nice." He held the door for me as I slipped out of the car.

"Yeah, it's pretty cool. My roommate's awesome. She's Kelly's sister-in-law."

Nixon bobbed his head. He'd met my cousin once, and her stunning model-like beauty had turned him into a thick-tongued mumbler. I'd hassled him about it for weeks, loving the red color of his cheeks. I'd never felt jealous or threatened, because although he thought Kelly was gorgeous, he could never fall for a girl like that. She was nothing like me.

Doubts gouged my insides as I thought of his office girl. She was nothing like me, either.

Shit, what if he stayed with her?

Swallowing back my fears, I rested my hand on his chest and caught his eye with a smile. "I'll always be yours. Being with anyone else just…" I let out a shaky laugh. "We're Chix, you know?"

With a gentle grin, he took my hand and kissed it. "I know."

My eyes glassed over, my smile growing wobbly. "I'll be here waiting for you."

"Okay," he croaked, his face flashing with agony as he let go of my hand.

He hated hurting people. He'd be dreading going to see Shayna.

"Take your time." I stepped against him and rested my hand on his cheek, trying to ease his unrest. "I'm not going anywhere."

My words made his eyes sparkle.

Brushing his knuckles down my cheek, he kissed me softly and then stepped back. His gaze told me he loved me as he walked to the car.

"See ya later, Nix."

He smiled before getting into the car and driving away.

I stood on the sidewalk until I couldn't see the rental car anymore. Letting out the breath I'd been holding, I did a nervous little chuckle and seriously wanted to twirl, but doubts held me steady.

What if he didn't do it?

"No," I whispered. "Don't think that way. Chix *will* be a thing again. It's meant to be."

I forced a quick twirl as if to prove I was right and then headed for the front door. The sudden implications of what we wanted to do didn't sink in until I reached the top of the stairs. There was no way we'd get back together problem-free. There were four years of history to unpack and build upon. I still had to tell Nixon the truth about his father's visit. And even though what felt like a millennium had passed, his father could still pull out some seriously dick moves.

At least we didn't need his money anymore. I had some savings. We could manage on that.

It wouldn't be easy, but it'd be worth it.

Doubt tickled my insides as my imagination built a solid case against me.

But I didn't want to let it win.

I wanted to be with Nixon!

"Screw you," I muttered to my dark meanderings as I opened the door.

I hadn't been strong enough to fight for us when I was just eighteen, but I was older and wiser. We'd work together to make his parents see the truth. Nixon and I were meant for each other. I could fit into his world if I wanted to. I could go to New York and live there while he studied law! A few years in a concrete jungle wouldn't kill me.

Maestro scampered into the living room before the door was even closed. His tail wagged excitedly as he greeted me.

"Hey, gorgeous boy." I crouched down to greet

him and scored a lick on the face.

I laughed and scratched him under the chin before standing tall and slipping the bag off my shoulder. It thumped to the floor just as Fliss appeared in the doorway. She had a wineglass in each hand and a sympathetic smile on her face.

"No need." I shook my head, determined to feed off my small thread of positivity.

"Really?" Her pale eyebrows shot up.

"Well, for one, it's lunchtime and way too early to crack open a wine bottle."

Fliss looked at the glasses, shrugged, then gulped down her portion.

I cracked up laughing as she licked her lips and said, "Yum!"

"You're unbelievable."

"I think the word you're looking for is amazing."

It was impossible not to love that girl.

"So, tell me why you're so happy." She walked to the couch and placed our wines on the coffee table.

"Because I had a wonderful trip home."

"You're a day early." Her expression was dry and skeptical.

"Because you were right." I cleared my throat and strolled to the couch. Going for casual would lighten what I was about to say.

"But of course." She grinned. "What am I right about?"

"He has a girlfriend."

She winced.

"And we got back early so that he can have a very serious discussion with her."

"Really?" Fliss gripped my arm and I nodded, unable to fight my grin. "No way, that's huge."

"I know." I bit my lip. "I don't envy what he's about to do, but… Shit, Fliss. This is everything I've been wanting!"

Her smile was sweet yet cautious.

"What?" I frowned.

"Nothing. I think it's great."

"No, you don't. What?"

"I'm just…" She tucked her hair behind her ear.

"What?" My voice grew low and stern.

"You left him…for what you swear are really good reasons. Do they not matter anymore?"

I looked down to my checkered pants and started tracing the boxes. "I'm not saying there aren't a few obstacles, but…" I blinked and nodded. "I really want him back, Fliss."

"I know," she whispered, rubbing my shoulder.

She was too much of a realist to truly celebrate with me. She wouldn't do that until Nixon was free of his relationship and officially mine again.

Leaning back with a sigh, I tuned into the soft strains of music coming from the kitchen—"Everything I Didn't Say."

Typical. Another sad song about broken relationships.

The frickin' music had been like a character of its own on my road trip. Every song a reminder of what I'd let slip through my fingers. Of what I still had to face in order to win the prize that had been snatched away from me too soon.

NINETEEN

NIXON

"Everything I Didn't Say" was playing on the radio as I drove back to my apartment near UCLA. I couldn't help questioning myself the closer I got to home. Had I said everything I should have to Charlie?

She still hadn't told me why she'd left in the first place, yet I was getting ready to dump the person who'd been loyal to me from the moment I met her.

It was a hard pill to swallow, and I seriously didn't know what to do with it.

Being with Charlie was magical. It always had been.

Then when she wasn't there reality hit again, and I was struggling to reenter it.

I was about to end the life I'd known for the last couple of years. It'd been a good life.

Not a magical one.

But a reliable one.

Biting my lips together, I slammed the wheel and tried to figure out what the hell I really wanted.

Charlie.

She always made me happy.

But being with her was also confusing—unchecked joy married with huge amounts of self-doubt that she'd get bored with me or spontaneously fly away on a breeze. I never wanted to be responsible for holding her back, which meant I had to let go of my own fears. My life had always been stable, certain. Being with Charlie meant I couldn't rely on that safety anymore. Would I ever find the courage to let go and truly be with her?

It would mean defying my parents—people I'd spent my life trying to please. I didn't want to hurt them. Not after everything they'd been through with losing Reagan.

Me being with Shayna made them so happy.

And she was a good woman.

I cared about her. I loved her.

She didn't set me free the way Charlie always did, but she was safe and trustworthy…and she deserved my loyalty. We'd been together for two years. I couldn't just turn my back on that because I felt like it.

Commitment meant something, and I couldn't hurt her.

But Charlie—somehow it always came back to her.

With a sad sigh, I parked outside our apartment and leaned my forehead against the wheel. For some weird reason I thought about snow.

My life had been turned upside down because of that random spring snowstorm. Thousands of tiny flakes, harmless on their own, but en masse they could shut down an airport…and change a life.

Leaning back, I gazed up at the house. Dread settled in my belly as I thought about what awaited me inside. Tears and heartbreak. I'd be the cause of it.

Exhaustion pulled at me, reminding me of how little sleep I'd had, how unprepared I was for any kind of argument or tears.

Charlie told me to take my time. She understood how hard it would be for me.

I still had one day of spring break left. Maybe in the morning, I'd have the energy and resilience to do what I needed to.

Poor Shayna.

I hadn't really admitted to Charlie how serious things were between us. She didn't know we were living together. All I'd said was that I had a girlfriend. There were so many different degrees within that relationship.

Guilt munched on my insides as I slithered out

of the car. My feet were concrete bricks as I climbed the front steps. I could hear giggling from inside and took a moment to steel myself before opening the door.

"Nixon!" My name was shouted in unison when I stepped into the living-dining area.

Shayna, Harper, Mimi, and my mother were sitting around our small dining table, lunch food spread between them.

"You're home early!" Shayna squealed and jumped up from the chair. Her arms were tight around my neck, her body familiar against mine. I gave her a squeeze before letting her go. "I was hoping you'd be back in time."

"You look exhausted," Mom said.

I looked over Shayna's shoulder and struggled to find my voice. "Mom."

She looked so happy, hanging out with Shayna and the girls. She'd been practically euphoric since Shayna and I started dating. She'd been the one to introduce us, to encourage me to ask out the stunning blonde. She was the cupid in our relationship, and her wings would fall right off if she knew what I was planning on doing.

She was genuinely happy these days, unhindered by the cloud of Reagan's death. Her son was doing well and she was flourishing in my success. All the good things that were happening to me meant the world to her.

Guilt added a few extra pounds onto my shoulders.

Dumping Shayna, hurting her so I could be with

the girl Mom never wanted me with…it would steal her smile in a heartbeat. Could I really do that to her?

"I didn't expect to see you here," I croaked.

"Well, Shayna invited me over." She giggled. "Your father's away and I figured I'd keep her company since you were taking so long to get back." Her motherly expression softened even more. "You look like you need some sleep."

Shayna let me go but snuggled into my side. I lightly squeezed her shoulder as she nestled her forehead into the crook of my neck. I kissed the top of her head without even thinking about it. "Yeah, I kind of drove through the night."

"Aw, to get back to your girl." Harper placed her hand on her heart, and all I could do was offer up a tight smile.

My girlfriend squeezed me around the middle.

"Shayna said you drove back with an old school friend?" Mom's eyebrows dipped and fear clutched my belly. "Who was it?"

I glanced down at Shayna, not sure what to say. I couldn't do it now. I couldn't break her heart in front of her friends. Sure, they'd be there to comfort her, but I wasn't quite brave enough to put myself in the line of fire.

Besides, Mom would be torn apart.

I had to be really careful how I played this.

"Um…" I licked my lips and decided to lie. Not a full-blown one, just a little whitey. "Chuck."

Mom's eyes bulged. "Chuck, as in Charlie?"

"No. Chuck, as in a guy in my statistics class. I

don't think you knew him." I scratched my eyebrow while I spoke, avoiding eye contact.

"Oh." Mom relaxed with a smile. "I thought you meant..." Her gaze drifted to Shayna, then flicked to mine.

"Nope." I shook my head and then forced a smile when Shayna looked up at me. "Anyway, I need to get some sleep before I fall over."

"Good idea." Shayna grinned. "I need you awake for tomorrow."

My forehead crinkled with a frown. "Tomorrow?"

"Yes." She wiggled her eyebrows. "I thought you wouldn't be back, but now you are and we can go together."

"To where?" I glanced at Mimi and Mom when they started laughing—a triumphant kind of snicker that made me nervous.

Shayna's tongue skimmed the side of her mouth, her eyes sparkling. "I'm going to surprise you."

"Oh, Nixon doesn't like surprises," Mom singsonged.

"Well, it's good for him to experience some." Shayna giggled and planted a kiss on my cheek. Mom tipped her head with an adoring smile.

"Don't worry, you're going to love it." She winked and sent me on my way with a pat to my cheek. "Sleep well, baby."

I lifted my bag and shuffled out of the room, my insides a churning wreck.

Mom's face when I said Chuck. Shit, I thought

she was going to pass out.

And Shayna…wanting to surprise me with something I'd love.

Whatever she had planned for tomorrow had her pumped, and I couldn't just break up with her on the cusp of that. I'd have to get through the day and then find the right moment to gently ease out of the relationship.

It felt weird.

We'd planned to go to New York together. I was her ticket there. She'd be gutted. And I hated the idea of causing her pain.

Plus, the ramifications of dumping her would have a flow-on effect that would last a lot longer than a short, painful breakup speech.

Maybe I shouldn't do it.

Maybe this whole road trip with Charlie had just been a surreal dream and I had to snap the hell out of it.

But…

"Chix," I whispered, flopping onto my bed and picturing blue hair dancing on the breeze.

TWENTY

CHARLIE

I pushed open the frosted glass door of *All About the Bride and Groom* and smiled when I spotted Sarah working over a massive table at the back. She had a pencil in her hand and was studying some sketches while her hips wiggled in time with "We Belong" by Sheppard.

I grinned. The song made me think of Nix.

Hell, everything was making me think of Nix, which was why I'd jumped when Sarah called me asking if I could come in for a chat. She and Justin had some more work lined up for me and I was happy to take it. I needed the distraction.

I glanced at the wall and smiled at one of the framed wedding photos I'd taken last spring. It was a favorite of mine—windswept veil, the groom brushing a lock of hair off the bride's face, dusky blue sky backdrop. The light had been frickin' amazing that day. The setting sun turned everything to golden magic, creating a spotlight on the couple.

It was an honor to have so much of my work featured in the front reception area. Man, Justin and Sarah had done well. It had taken them a few years, but they finally saved up enough to lease a bigger place so they didn't have to run their business from home anymore. The two of them worked like dogs, but they both loved what they did and were so happy hanging out together that they didn't seem to mind.

It reminded me of my relationship with Nixon, and I was yet again struck by how right we were for each other. Sheppard backed me up by singing, "We belong together..."

I hummed along as I made my way into the back of the store.

I wasn't sure how long Nixon would take to break up with his girlfriend, but I wasn't above admitting that I'd be waiting by the phone for him.

Shit. I jerked to a stop.

I hadn't given him my number.

I grimaced until I realized that he knew where I lived and if he felt the same way I did, he'd be careening around to my door the second he broke up with Shayna.

It felt kind of weird thinking that. Like poor Shayna was being hurt so we could find our happiness.

But we'd been living without for years. It was our turn.

Right?

I pressed my hands to my stomach, trying to squash my doubts. The idea that he still might not go through with it wouldn't leave me alone.

My biggest hope was that she was just a casual girlfriend. He had said that it *could* get serious, not that it actually was.

I was so relieved I didn't have anyone to end things with. I'd been a free spirit…for a very good reason. My spirit—my heart—belonged to Nixon, and I couldn't imagine anyone else ever claiming it. And no one else would because soon enough, Nixon would be mine again.

Dumping my bag on a free chair, I turned to find Justin making coffees.

"Hey, Charlie. How are ya?" Not even a stutter; the guy was obviously relaxed today.

"Great." I smiled and realized that I actually was great. For the first time in a long time, I was excited about the future again. Plans buzzed inside of me. Dreams unfurled again as I imagined what I'd say to Nixon when he came knocking on my door.

"So how was your trip back?" Sarah grinned at me and then kissed Justin's cheek when he passed her a coffee.

He pointed at me. "D-do you want one?"

"No, I'm good." I brushed a hand through the air and slid my hands into my pockets. "Trip was good. I love traveling across this country. We had a blast. Better than waiting in a snowy airport anyway."

"Absolutely!" Sarah's bright eyes danced. "I love how spontaneous you are." Her new cut bangs rustled as she shook her head, then sipped her coffee.

"So, did you guys like the pictures I sent?"

"Love them." Sarah beckoned me toward her work space. "Justin's already played around on Photoshop. Check these out."

I stood next to her and leaned in to peruse Justin's handiwork. He'd superimposed the couple into my settings to help inspire Sarah's dress designs.

"Wow," I laughed. "That looks cool." I slid some pages around and unearthed a few of Sarah's sketches. "Has the future bride seen these yet?"

"No, she's coming in tomorrow. But I'm hoping she'll go for this sleek one."

"I love that." Man, she was good. Not only did the couple plan weddings, but Sarah designed and made the dresses too. She was a freaking genius. "That dress will look so amazing in photos. And that setting. With that light." My voice rose with enthusiasm the more I soaked in the concept. "We could put a cross processing filter on some of these too. Check it." I slid the pictures around and pointed out the colors that would come to life with a little manipulation. It'd give the couple a series of edgy shots that would look like they came straight out of a fashion magazine.

"They're going to go crazy over these. I can't wait to show them." Sarah did her happy dance, making Justin chuckle and gaze at her with an adoration that only he could.

He was such a romantic sap.

I laughed at him and shook my head.

He grinned. "We've convinced them to go for that Italian place you checked out for us. It'll be perfect for what they want."

"Will the ceremony be there too?"

"No, they want Central Park, so we're w-working out logistics to make that happen."

"Thankfully it's a really small, intimate wedding, so at least we're not dealing with huge numbers." Sarah blew out a breath, making her bangs dance up.

"They must love you guys. Turning their crazy dreams into reality."

"Yeah, well we love doing it, so..." Sarah shrugged.

"I've already booked you in for those dates, right?" Justin caught my attention and I headed over to his work space. He was pulling up Calendar on his computer.

I grabbed my phone and checked it. "Yup, I've got that locked in for late May already."

"Great. And we have a new job that just came in. It'll be for June, although we need to confirm exact dates."

"Okay." I tapped my phone screen, making a

note to be available in June.

The door opened at the front of the store and I stepped aside so Sarah could brush past me and greet her clients.

"Hello." Her voice was so bright and cute when she was trying to impress.

"Hi. It's nice to finally meet you." The bride had a strong, confident voice.

"I know." Sarah laughed. "We've spoken so much on the phone this week. It's nice to put a face to your lovely voice."

"Aw, thank you. We're so excited to be here."

I peered around the corner to get a glimpse of the couple.

And the ground beneath my feet suddenly turned into a gaping chasm that wanted to swallow me whole.

The woman with the strong, confident voice was standing next to Nixon.

My Nixon.

Holding his hand, squeezing his arm and staring lovingly into his eyes.

He grinned down at her and she leaned up to kiss him.

He didn't pull away or do that awkward laugh of his—the one where you couldn't figure out if he was clearing his throat or snickering.

No, he just stood there and let her lips press against his.

Sarah made an "aww" sound that made bile surge up my throat.

I swallowed the burning sensation, willing my

riotous stomach to calm the hell down.

"Well, why don't you two come through and we can get to work on planning your wedding. Your timing's perfect actually, because the photographer I want for you has just popped in." Sarah glanced over her shoulder, searching for me. I quickly stepped out of sight, nearly knocking Justin off his feet.

"Whoa, are you okay?" He steadied us both against the counter, gently rubbing my lower back.

"Yeah." I nodded, stepping out of his reach.

It was a total lie.

I wasn't anything near okay.

My heart was in pieces on the floor, and there'd be no king's horses or men to come and put the pieces back together.

Because Nixon, *my* Nixon, didn't just have a casual girlfriend…

He had a fiancée.

One he obviously had no intention of dumping because he was standing in a frickin' wedding planner's store ready to *get to work*!

TWENTY-ONE

NIXON

I felt bad smiling at Shayna…for going along with this crazy plan.

Shit. I shouldn't have even let her walk us into the store. Of all the surprises she could've dumped on me.

All About the Bride and Groom.

We weren't even officially engaged.

We'd talked about getting married in LA before moving to New York. Starting the next chapter as a married couple seemed to please everybody, so I'd just kind of let it ride. I'd even nodded when Dad had suggested he look for a ring on his trip to

Europe. He'd said it so casually that I hadn't really let it sink in.

I hadn't kicked up a fuss because I'd had no reason to.

It was before the snowstorm.

Before Charlie.

I didn't know what to do.

Shayna was so excited. How did I break her heart?

How did I stop this freight train?

How did I get what I wanted without hurting everybody in the process?

I'd worked my butt off trying to be the perfect son and boyfriend to avoid any more unhappiness.

Did I seriously have a right to just selfishly push all that aside?

The war within me raged, silent and undetected by those around me.

I couldn't give away my aching uncertainty. Not in the middle of the bridal store, with the pretty blonde lady smiling at me.

I shook her hand when Sarah introduced herself, then swallowed when she ushered us through to the offices. It was a nice place, white framed pictures on the walls, white furniture with a golden inlay. Very wedding-like.

If Shayna had her way, we'd be in one of those pictures. Me in a penguin suit, her looking gorgeous in a designer gown. She'd make a stunning bride. Diamonds in her hair, and heels. That's what she'd go for. High, sparkly heels—ankle breakers—but her ankles never turned. I didn't know how she did it, but her hips would sway and somehow keep her balanced. It was the first thing I noticed about her when we met, her high heels. My eyes had tracked up her body and it was the first time I'd felt something since losing Charlie.

Maybe that was why I'd let my parents push me into a relationship with her. It was something to take the dull edge off my miserable existence.

Shayna wasn't what I thought I wanted—blonde, sleek, classy in every sense of the word. But she'd grown on me, and I'd learned to love the little things that made her who she was. Like the fact that she was loyal and dependable, and quite happy to organize my life for me.

Our fathers worked together, and when they spotted the tiniest spark between Shayna and me, they put a master plan in place. Both high-flying lawyers who wanted the best for their kids, they worked behind the scenes to make sure Shayna and I kept meeting up and falling into opportunities to get to know each other. Then Mom got to work, encouraging me to ask Shayna out. Together our parents were a force to be reckoned with, but they were all good friends and they loved that their precious children had fallen for each other.

Being with Shayna made a lot of people happy.

Breaking up with Shayna would make a lot of people heartbroken.

The hairs on the back of my neck prickled as I was pulled further into the wedding maze. "Let Me Down Easy" by Sheppard was playing in the background, but it wasn't until I rounded the corner that I truly understood why.

Music had been cursing me ever since New York, and it wasn't going to stop just because I was back in LA.

"So, I'd like you to meet Justin." Sarah pointed to her partner. He stepped forward and shook Shayna's hand. He reached for mine, but I was struggling to move.

Because all I could see was blue-tipped hair, trembling lips and these sad hazel eyes.

"And this is one of our photographers, Charlie."

"Hi." Shayna's enthusiasm made me wince. Stepping forward, she took Charlie's hand and shook it, gushing about how important photos were for capturing the day and making it last forever.

Charlie nodded like a robot, her hand still locked within Shayna's.

They were touching. My past and my present were meeting face-to -face, and I felt like my life was about to end.

"Nice to meet you." Charlie's voice sounded dead and mechanical, so unlike her.

Justin gave her an odd look before smiling at me and shaking my hand. "We're really excited for this w-wedding."

"Thank you," I somehow managed.

"I've already had so many ideas." Sarah beamed. "Based on our conversations this week, I've come up with a concept I think you're going to love. I can't wait to show you guys."

Sarah led us back to a meeting room while Justin offered us a drink. I declined and Shayna asked for an espresso.

"Charlie, can you join us for this meeting?" Sarah asked, then winked at me and Shayna. "She's got a great eye and so many artistic ideas. You're going to love her."

Shayna shone me an ecstatic smile and I wanted to throw up. Pulling out a chair for Shayna, I caught Charlie's eye across the table. She just stared at me, her jaw clenched tight.

We hadn't shaken hands yet. We'd settled for a polite nod across the room, pretending like we were meeting for the first time.

It was weird and majorly awkward.

I gave her an agonized frown, desperate to somehow explain, but I couldn't do that in front of Shayna and two people we'd only just met. I wasn't a complete asshole—I was a confused one.

The table was covered in rough sketches and a big sheet of paper that had obviously been used for brainstorming. The words 'lavish' and 'elegant' struck me first and I swallowed, my throat swelling thicker by the second.

I took a seat beside Shayna, who immediately grabbed my hand and gave it a squeeze.

"We're so super excited for this."

Sarah grinned. "I bet you've been dreaming about this day since you were a little girl."

"How'd you know?" She giggled. "Every bride-to-be probably says that to you."

"I notice you don't have a ring." Charlie took a

seat beside Sarah.

Shayna laughed, then leaned against me. "It's coming. Nixon's father is bringing it back from Europe. I found the most stunning ring, and it's got this amazing story behind it."

I glanced at Shayna, giving her a tight smile. Shit, I didn't even know that.

She was oblivious to my confusion as she told Sarah all about the history behind the precious ring and how it used to belong to some gentry from her distant past.

"The ring is being redesigned, of course, but the original diamond will be the main feature."

"Wow, that's so amazing." Sarah's eyes sparkled with enthusiasm. "And it will fit perfectly with the themes we've discussed."

"I know." Shayna's voice pitched high. Her smile had never been brighter.

"You know, most brides have pretty clear ideas of what they want, but yours are crystal. I think we're going to work really well together." Sarah tapped her iPad, then turned to me. "So, Nixon. I know what Shayna wants out of this wedding, but what do you want? It's your day too, and I think it's really important that the groom has some say."

"Oh, I…"

Shayna gave me an expectant eyebrow raise when I glanced at her.

My eyes shot back to Charlie, but her glowering look made them shoot straight back to Sarah. She seemed the safest bet.

I opened my mouth to speak but couldn't come

up with anything intelligent.

I didn't know. I didn't…care.

Which made me feel really bad. I should have cared. It was my wedding. It was a huge deal.

But…

We weren't even engaged!

And if Charlie had her way, I'd be breaking up with Shayna any day now.

Which was what I wanted too, right?

Not right that second, but…

I mean…

I opened my mouth to formulate the kind of response I knew Shayna would want to hear, then finally blurted a lame, "Oh, you know. Happy wife, happy life. I want whatever Shayna does."

Charlie rolled her eyes, looking ready to melt something with her laser glare.

Shayna gave me a sweet smile and squeezed my hand again.

Sarah hesitated, her blue eyes stripping me bare with the briefest look. "Most grooms want a little something of themselves represented on the day. Why don't you have a think about it and let us know when you come up with something that epitomizes Nixon."

I let out a breathy laugh, about to agree with her because that's what she wanted to hear, but the words evaporated in my mouth when I caught Charlie's pained expression. Shit, it was way worse than her glare. Anger somehow seemed easier to deal with than heartbreak.

Looking down at the table, I focused on the one

square of glossy white I could see beneath all the paperwork.

The door opened and Justin walked in with an espresso for Shayna.

"S-sorry for taking so long. I had trouble with the m-m-machine."

"No stress, babe." Sarah gave him a kind smile.

He relaxed beneath her gaze, and for a second I wondered what that felt like. To be with a girl who put you at ease. Shayna made me tense with her silent demands and expectations. Charlie made me nervous because I never knew what she was going to do next.

Rubbing my forehead, I leaned back in my chair and tried to figure out how I was going to survive the rest of the meeting.

Swallowing the boulder in my throat, I tuned in to Shayna and Sarah's conversation. They were both talking brightly, getting more and more excited as ideas bubbled between them.

My mind quickly wandered though, my eyes tracking to Charlie. She was listening with this bland look on her face. Her lips were turned down at the corners and she was blinking more than usual.

Averting my gaze, I focused on the shiny white table and caught wisps of the music playing softly through the speakers.

"Let Me Down Easy" by Sheppard had started up again for some weird reason.

But then maybe it wasn't weird, because music seemed to be playing some kind of role in my tortured life. As if proving my point, Charlie's eyes flicked to mine and I knew she was listening to the song as well.

The people around us turned to fuzzy blurs in my peripherals and all I could see was Charlie, the way her eyes glassed with emotion. The tendon in her neck strained tight and her nostrils flared as she desperately tried to hold it all in.

I wanted to reach across the table and grab her hand, rub my thumb across her knuckles and comfort her. But how could I when my current girlfriend was sitting next to me gushing wedding plans?

I'd made Charlie believe that I was in no more than an uncertain relationship.

She had no idea Shayna and I lived together.

She didn't know what she was asking me to walk away from…and how much that would hurt people. I should have told her.

Would it have made a difference?

Would she still have wanted me if she knew just how committed I was?

Someone cleared her throat, snapping everything back into focus.

I shuffled in my seat and glanced at Shayna, who was looking at me expectantly.

"Those were the dates we were thinking, right?"

"Uh-huh." I nodded, not even sure what dates we were talking about.

"Can you book those in, Charlie?" Justin shot her a glance, then had to tap her arm before she'd look at him. "The last Saturday in June."

"Uh…yeah, um… Let me…" She pulled out her phone and tapped her thumb over the screen. Her eyes darted to me, then across to Shayna, then back to me.

"O-h, let me down easy." The singers' voices rang in harmony, the background music making my skin prickle.

Glancing down at her phone, Charlie bit her lips together and shook her head. "I'm so sorry. I can't do those dates."

TWENTY-TWO

CHARLIE

Why wasn't Nixon standing up and dumping office girl on the spot?

Why wasn't he shouting out that this wasn't what he wanted?

He was just sitting there, planning his fucking wedding.

I couldn't do it.

I couldn't watch him marry someone else.

When "Let Me Down Easy" started randomly playing again, I took it as a sign.

It was time to go. To walk away yet again so my best friend could find the happiness he so obviously wanted.

"You can't make those dates?" Sarah looked a mixture of surprised and disappointed.

"I'm really sorry." I cleared my throat and rechecked my phone to really sell whatever lie I was trying to come up with. "When Justin asked me before, he didn't have a set date, and these guys arrived before I could tell you."

"Tell us what?" Sarah forced a smile at her clients before staring back at me.

"That I'm actually not going to be here at the end of June."

Justin's dark eyebrows dipped together. "Wh-where are you going to be?"

My jaw worked to the side, trembling just a little as I spat out the first lie that came to me. "I haven't had a chance to discuss it with you guys yet, but I'm making plans to leave LA, so I'm not going to be here for this wedding."

Sarah closed her eyes and I knew she was thinking, "Not again!"

I turned to the future bride and groom, focusing solely on the bride because if I thought of Nixon as a groom, I was going to throw up my heart. "I'm so sorry. But I'll hook you up with Kaine. He's an amazing photographer. I promise, you'll love his work. He does some fashion photography, and he'll totally be able to set you guys up with exactly what you want."

Sarah caught my eye and gave me an irritated frown before pasting on a confident smile for her clients. "I know you fell in love with Charlie's stuff on our website, but let me grab the laptop and I'll go through some of Kaine's shots. Charlie's right, he really is fantastic."

Jerking out of my chair, I rushed to the door and opened it for Sarah. "I'll call him right now."

"Okay." She gave me a tight smile.

Clenching my jaw, I turned to look at both Nixon and Shayna. It took every ounce of maturity I possessed, but I forced a smile and said, "Good luck with your wedding."

I have no idea what Nixon's face did; I turned before I could take in his expression.

Justin's gaze followed me out the door, I could feel it. He knew as well as Nixon that my pants were on fire, but he was nice enough not to say anything.

Ducking around the corner, I sent a quick text to Kaine, not trusting my voice to talk to anyone in more than short sentences.

Sarah brushed past me with the computer in her hands. "You have some explaining to do after this," she whispered.

"I'm sorry," I mumbled. "It's kind of last minute."

"As in *literally* the last minute." Sarah stopped and gave me a confused frown. "I know you like to take off at the drop of a hat, but when you got back in touch last year, you gave me the impression that you'd be around for a long time. You said you were committed. You said I could book you in months ahead because you were sticking around this time."

My gaze darted to the floor.

"Come on, Charlie. What's going on?"

"I'm sorry I'm letting you down." I swallowed, then was saved by my beeping phone. I read the screen and sagged with relief. "Kaine can do it."

"It won't be the same as you," Sarah grumbled. Hugging the laptop against her chest, she gave me a sad smile. "Are you seriously leaving again?"

My throat swelled as I gazed into her sweet blue eyes.

I couldn't nod or shake. I didn't know.

I'd never felt so lost and uncertain, even when Nixon's father had ordered me out of his son's life.

Giving my arm a quick squeeze, Sarah kissed my cheek. "I've got to get back in there, the meeting's finishing soon. But I need the whole story before I'm willing to say goodbye to my best photographer. You got it?"

Her firm, mother-like expression made me nod.

"I'm gonna go."

"You don't want to say goodbye first?" She pointed toward the meeting room.

"I can't." The words came out in a choking whisper. Before she could question me any more, I grabbed my bag and turned for the door.

The second I burst into the sunlight it hit me full force.

"He's getting married." The words popped out of my mouth, bringing with them an ugly realization that made my knees buckle. I stumbled forward and caught myself before landing on the concrete, trying to turn my gawky trip into a smooth walk. It didn't work. I looked like an idiot but was too dazed to even care.

"He's getting married." The words wobbled out of me, wispy and pathetic.

My insides crawled with panic, breaths punching out of me. I suddenly felt completely lost. It was the weirdest feeling, like my world was tipping on its axis as I was faced with the one scenario I'd never even thought to consider.

"He's getting married!" I yelled, scaring the lady who just happened to be bustling past me.

She yelped and gave me a sharp frown before marching away.

Clutching my stomach, I spun and ran down the street, careening around the corner in this blind haze. I didn't know what to do or where to run.

All I could see was Nixon waiting at the end of the aisle for some bride.

But not me!

Some girl I didn't even know was going to slip a ring on his finger and claim him for life! And there was me foolishly thinking that she was just a girlfriend. You know, nothing too serious. They'd break up and he'd show up on my doorstep.

But how could I expect him to break up with his fiancée?

"His fiancée," I whimpered, pressing the back of my hand against my lips.

Scrambling for my phone, I quickly unlocked the screen and tried to call Fliss. I needed to speak to someone before I fell apart on a public street. I was acting like a freaking crazy person, fighting tears and hyperventilating. I'd even frickin' run the opposite direction of my car. But I couldn't go back and get it because I might bump into Nixon and his future wife!

This couldn't be happening.

Was life seriously bitch-slapping me for what I did four years ago?

I thought I was getting my second chance!

Instead I was being mocked. Fooled into believing that everything I wanted was coming back, only to have it completely ripped out of my hands one day later.

"Shit," I muttered as Fliss's voice mail message kicked in. Pulling up my contacts, I scrolled through until I spotted Kelly's name and pressed it.

"Hey," she answered with a smile in her voice. "How's it going?"

"Where are you?" I clipped.

"Uh…out to lunch. Are you okay?"

"I need to talk to someone, stat."

Her voice dropped with concern. "What's up?"

"He's getting married!" I screeched. "And I'm shouting into my phone in the middle of a public street! Help me!"

"Whoa, okay. I'm with Marcus and some friends at La Saveur. I can—"

"I know that place!" I yelled. "See you in a minute."

"No, wait—"

I hung up before she could tell me not to come. Crazy lady had fully taken over as I ran down the street, jumping around people and not stopping until I reached the restaurant, a puffing, panting mess.

Kelly and Marcus were at an outside table with a couple I vaguely recognized.

They were all leaning in, chatting together and looking kind of worried when I approached the table and announced, "He's getting married."

"Okay." Kelly grabbed my arm and pulled me down to squat beside her. "Just breathe for a second."

"Here, take this chair." The guy with an English accent offered me a friendly smile before pulling out the chair adjacent to him.

He was so familiar. I'd totally met him before but couldn't remember where.

I slid onto the seat and clutched the edges while he shared a quick look with the redhead beside him. She was familiar too.

They both had rings on their fingers.

Had I taken photos at their wedding?

Shit, I was disturbing a couple's lunch.

The thought hit me like a bazooka to the chest.

It seemed that everyone around me was married or getting married, and me, Miss Free Spirit, was stuck all alone pining for someone who'd just been snatched out of my grasp.

Marcus caught my eye and gave me a gentle smile. "I take it you're having a bad day."

"Pretty much." My head bobbed erratically.

Kelly's eyes darted to the couple. She gave them an awkward smile before looking back at me. "Do you want to talk about it? We can go for a walk or something."

"No, it's okay. I shouldn't disturb your lunch, I just..."

"It's alright." The redhead smiled at me. "We're waiting for our friends anyway, so you're really not disturbing anyone."

"I'm Harry, by the way." The man beside me stuck out his hand, then pointed over his shoulder. "And this is my lovely Jane."

She grinned and shook my hand once I'd let his go.

"Nice to meet you," I whispered.

"We have actually met before." Jane poured me a glass of water and set it down in front of me. "You work with my best friend, Sarah."

"Oh." My hands trembled as I reached for the glass, suddenly picturing Harry and Jane's faces at *All About the Bride and Groom.* "Nice to see you again."

My words were feeble and drowned out by the glass of water. I gulped it back, then wiped a drip of water off my chin. I nearly dropped the glass as I put it back on the table.

Harry steadied it for me, his kind expression sweet enough to make me cry.

My eyes began to burn and my nose tingled with the onset of tears.

"So...who's getting married?" Marcus's eyebrows rose while my shoulders deflated.

"Nixon. He was..." I sighed.

"Your best friend from high school." Kelly's smile was soft and sweet, her blue gaze lighting with a realization she'd probably known ever since

I introduced them.

"I'm supposed to be taking the photos for his wedding," I blubbered. "They're meeting with Justin and Sarah right now."

Jane's smile was soft and sympathetic. "So that's why they're late. We're waiting for Justin and Sarah to join us for lunch."

"Of course you are." My voice trailed off as I gazed around the four of them sitting there with their lunch wine and looking so incredibly grown up and normal.

I would never be that.

Which was probably why Nixon was getting married to someone else. He didn't want to hurt my feelings so he just quietly left me on the sidewalk, with no intention of ever showing up on my doorstep.

He'd moved on.

And sure, we may have gotten hot and heavy there for a second, but that was just the heat of the moment. I wasn't enough to make him want to change his life.

"Sweetie." Kelly rubbed my arm. "I thought you lost contact with him years ago. I know you always liked him, but...was he more than just a friend?"

My jaw trembled as I opened my mouth to speak but found nothing to say.

"You kept that pretty quiet," Kelly murmured.

"I couldn't tell anyone." I dipped my head. "We hooked up the summer after graduation."

"No, you went to Montana."

"Before I left." I swallowed. "It was perfect and

then…I realized it couldn't stay that way. The consequences of us being together were too big, so I kind of freaked out and left."

Harry and Jane shared this sad smile, like they understood something I didn't.

"At the time, I was so justified and it made sense. I thought I was doing him this big favor, but deep down I always hoped that when the timing was right, life would somehow bring us back together. And it did!" I sucked in a breath. "We met up in New York last week, during a freaking spring snowstorm! A totally random bumping into each other thing and I thought…I thought…maybe. You know?"

"But he's getting married," Kelly whispered.

My face crumpled with despair and I covered my eyes to try to ward off the tears. I didn't want to cry again.

"I'm so sorry, Chuck." Marcus sounded like he really was. Fliss would say exactly the same thing when I saw her. She'd be sympathetic and sweet, just like her brother.

And the words would sting just as bad when she said them, because it wouldn't fix my problem.

Slapping the back of my hand onto my thigh, I looked at them and in a desperate whine asked, "Is it seriously so farfetched to think that you can meet your true love in high school? Am I that naive?"

"Justin and Sarah met in their first year of college." Jane's smile was etched with sadness. "They hit a few bumps along the way and broke up for a while, but you don't give up on your soul mate."

"Soul mates. Yes!" I snapped my fingers and pointed at her. "That's what I'm talking about. You believe in them, then? That's good! And you guys…" I turned to Kelly and pointed between her and Marcus. "Yeah, of course you do. It's Marcus! He's totally your soul mate. So what do you do if your soul mate thinks he should be with this other girl?"

Harry's face was etched with empathy. "You know, it's possible to love more than once. I do believe in soul mates, but life doesn't always work out the way you want it to. And so it gifts you something else." He turned to Jane and smiled at her. "Something that's exactly what you need."

Jane's expression melted with affection and she leaned her cheek on his shoulder. He kissed her forehead and I turned away because I couldn't stomach that answer. I didn't want life to give me anything else! I wanted Nixon!

And I couldn't have him!

The thought was a brutal punch that hurt my already wounded soul. Jerking out of my seat, I hitched my bag onto my shoulder. "I'm sorry for disturbing your lunch. Thanks for hearing me out."

"Hey, I can take you home." Kelly went to rise from her chair, but I gently pushed her back down.

"It's okay. You enjoy your lunch. I need to go get my car, and…" I sighed, shaking my head at the lack of answers I was finding.

And what?

I didn't know.

My entire day was now a blank nothingness. I couldn't think past my shock or hollow despair.

"See you later." I gave Harry and Jane a glum smile before easing away from the table.

"Bye, Charlie." Jane tinkled her fingers with a sad smile.

"Can you not..." I shook my head. "Can you not say anything to Sarah and Justin? It's bad enough that I just spewed all this to you guys."

Harry grinned. "Your secret's safe with us."

"Thanks," I mumbled, and walked away.

"Call me when you get home." Kelly's voice chased after me. I raised my hand to acknowledge her but didn't know if I'd find the guts to talk anymore.

The way I felt was worse than when I'd left Nixon in the first place. Back then I'd been walking away for his sake. So noble. I was saving his family.

But this time was different. I was being forced away because he'd moved on. His choice, not mine.

I had to somehow come to terms with the fact that being with Nixon was nothing more than a pipe dream.

He wouldn't be dumping his fiancée to be with me. He'd found the normal life he deserved. The one his parents so desperately wanted for him. The one he obviously wanted too.

When I turned the corner, I spotted Sarah and Justin walking down the street toward La Saveur. They were holding hands and grinning at each other. I didn't want to get caught in another conversation, so I quickly ducked across the street and ran back to my car the long way.

Slamming the door of my beat-up VW Beetle shut, I shoved my key in the ignition and revved the engine. Music blasted through the speakers, amplified by the fact that all my windows were up.

"Empty" by The Click Five reverberated around me.

I should have just turned it off, but the silence would have been worse, so I let it play.

It took me home on a wave of sadness that was heavy and debilitating. I never thought I'd be one of those sappy girls who felt torn apart by a broken heart. But there it was. Four years of wistful hope was worthless, because Nixon was getting married and there was no longer a chance of Chix ever being a thing again.

TWENTY-THREE

NIXON

I was tortured. It'd been two days since I last saw Charlie and I couldn't get her out of my head.

But I needed to.

Or I needed to break up with Shayna.

I closed my eyes, nausea rolling through me as I drove the streets, taking the longest way home that I could.

When I was with Charlie—kissing her, reliving the past—it was so easy to dream again. To imagine this perfect existence.

But it wouldn't be perfect.

I'd have to hurt Shayna and my family in order

to get it.

I'd have to break hearts and then risk having my own broken all over again.

What if Charlie left me without a word?

She was impulsive and spontaneous. Backing out of the June wedding? She'd done that on the fly. But knowing her, she'd go through with leaving LA.

Because she was Charlie.

Unpredictable Charlie Watson.

A wisp on a breeze.

Mom always said she wasn't right for me. I'd fought so hard to prove her wrong, but then Charlie had done exactly what Mom said she would.

And so had Shayna. She'd been loyal, trustworthy and loving.

My parents wanted me to marry a gorgeous, reliable person who would give me a good, stable life. They wanted that because they loved me. They'd helped me get it.

Was I willing to just throw that all away because I felt like it?

That didn't make sense.

Love was a choice.

So, which woman did I choose to love for the rest of my life?

When I first got back to LA, I was flying high, ready to end things with Shayna and start fresh with Charlie. But then reality hit—consequences, doubts, uncertainty, fear.

My mind was telling me one thing loud and

clear. I knew what the right choice was, but I didn't know if I had the courage to let go of the other.

Would Charlie haunt me forever?

I signaled left and turned down a street, not realizing until I was halfway down that I was driving past Charlie's house. I slammed on the brakes and just sat in the middle of the road, staring up at her door.

My fingers gripped the wheel so tightly my knuckles turned white.

"What do you want from this moment, man? Are you knocking on her door to say…what? Fucking what!" I thumped the wheel and pulled into a parking space down the street when I noticed a beat-up VW Beetle coming down the road behind me.

Agitation made my fingers jitter. I tapped them on the wheel and stared out the windshield. My jaw kept clenching and unclenching while a new song started on the radio.

I didn't even register the music until the beat kicked in. Finger clicks grabbed my attention and I stared down at the radio. "11 Blocks" by Wrabel. I knew the song, not word perfect, but enough to know the gist. Some poor loser still stuck on a girl, struggling to let her go when he had a perfectly amazing woman waiting for him at home.

With a heavy sigh, I leaned back against my seat and forced my brain to function logically.

When Charlie first left me, I'd fallen into this morose melancholy funk. Listening to sad-ass music all the time, speaking in mumbles and grunts. She stole me, turned me back into the boy who'd lost his beloved older sister.

So I threw myself into studies…and then I met Shayna.

Shayna pulled me out of my shell and took the edge off. She made it better…and she stuck around.

Surely she was the right choice.

Logic figured it all out for me, but this wave of resistance kept pounding my heart.

I thought I'd given up Charlie. I thought I'd set myself free of her, but I was right back where I started. Because in reality she still owned a piece of me.

"Make up your fucking mind, man! Or just get out of here!" I glanced over my shoulder as I reached for my keys, and froze.

Charlie was standing at the bottom of her steps, staring across the street…at me.

I couldn't just take off. I'd never deny I was coward, but that really was going too far.

With a heavy sigh, I shunted the door open with my shoulder and walked across the road.

Charlie tensed and took a step back, creating a bigger gap between us.

"Hey." I greeted her with a feeble wave.

Her nostrils flared. The bag of groceries in her hand made a crinkling sound as she gripped the bottom corner.

"I have to assume you're not here for the reasons I want you to be, so you should just say your goodbyes and go." Her eyes flashed with anger. "Your fiancée is no doubt wondering where you are."

I scratched my chin and let out a cynical huff. "She's not even my fiancée yet. It's not official."

"Well, you should probably do something about that, because I think she's pretty set on planning your June wedding!" She huffed, her fingers trembling as she rubbed her forehead and looked away from me. "You made me think it wasn't that serious, but...you're getting married!"

"I..." I groaned and squeezed my eyes shut, already hating the conversation.

"What do you want, Nix? Huh? What? Why are you here?" she shouted.

"Hey, don't yell at me," I snapped. "This is your fault!"

"Mine?" Her eyebrows dipped together.

"You left me. *You* left without even the courtesy of an explanation and expected me to what? Just wait around on the off-chance you might change your mind and come back? You obviously didn't love me enough to stay in the first place, and the last four years didn't inspire you to track me down! Of course I was going to move on!"

Her face blanched white like I'd just slapped her or something. But I was on a roll so I kept going, finally spewing out all the angst I'd been carrying for far too long.

"You know, I held off making a move on you for two years because I was petrified I'd lose my best friend if I did. But then we went camping that summer and you made me believe. You fooled me into thinking we could have something amazing.

And I will never understand why you did that. Why? Why did you do that to me? And why, when I'm around you, do you make it so fucking easy to forget that you did that to me?"

My voice quavered like I was about to cry. It made me pathetic and un-manly, but what did I really have to lose? A big chunk of my heart was finally breaking off. It'd been teetering on the edge for years anyway, rotting and festering. But finally saying it out loud like that… The chunk fell away, splashing into the ocean of pain I'd been living with ever since she took off to Montana.

Tears lined her lashes, sparking that torturous doubt that confused me. Why was she crying? Why did she keep acting like she cared?

"You thought I fooled you?" she whispered.

"Well, I don't know what else to think." I threw my arms wide. "I thought we were in love and you just left." My voice hitched and I looked to the ground, cupping the back of my head.

Dammit. I was not going to fucking cry!

My eyes burned as I listened to the sound of Charlie placing her groceries on the step and walking down to stand beside me.

She placed her hand on top of mine and pressed her forehead into my cheek.

I should have moved away but I couldn't. Especially when she started talking in that trembling whisper.

"I…I wasn't right for you, Nix. I would have held you back. And I knew if I tried to tell you that to your face, I wouldn't have had the courage. My selfishness would've won. I had to leave the way I did or I wouldn't have been able to. You deserved so much better than me. I just wanted you to be happy."

My face buckled with confusion. It took me a moment to process what she was saying. When I pulled back and stared down at her, tears were trailing down her cheeks. I had to fight the urge to brush them away.

"You left to make *me* happy?" I touched my chest.

"I definitely didn't leave to make me happy. I've missed you every day." She sniffed and swiped at her tears. "My life will never be as great as it was then."

"I don't—" Pinching the bridge of my nose, I huffed again. My brain was going to explode in a second. Her logic was unreasonable. She left to make me happy? Was she insane?

"How would you leaving me make my life better? How would that make me happy!" My shout rose to an uncharacteristic roar.

She flinched and took a small step away from me. "I wasn't good enough for you. I'm too wild and unpredictable. Your parents—" She pressed her lips together and looked to the ground.

"What? My parents what?"

She sighed and bunched her hair at the nape of her neck. "They didn't want us together. We both knew that. It would've been too hard. With the whole Reagan thing, I didn't want to cause a rift or destroy family ties. They need you. They love you, and you deserve... You shouldn't have to fight. I would've disrupted everything. You're too smart and talented to end up with the likes of me. I would have led you astray and...and ruined your life!"

What the hell was she saying?

Did she think...?

I shook my head, confusion making my frown deep and painful. "You thought you were doing me a favor?"

Her expression buckled as a fresh set of tears lined her lashes. "They're the only family you have. I couldn't drive a wedge between you. They're your blood."

"And you were my heart." I closed the gap between us, grabbing her face and pressing my forehead against hers. "You were my heart."

TWENTY-FOUR

CHARLIE

Those sweet words tore a sob right out of me. I buckled against him, gripping his sweater as he wrapped his arms around me and held on tight.

I wanted him to never let go.

But saying all that, stating the truth that way, made me realize that I'd left for a reason.

I may have felt bullied into that reason, but it was still a valid one.

He said I was his heart, but I wasn't anymore. He'd given it to someone else.

Nixon had a family who would be devastated if he left that perfect woman for me. I'd just end up doing what I was trying to avoid in the first place.

And yes, Nixon was close to graduating, so I wouldn't be robbing him of an education. But there was still law school to go, and I was pretty sure his parents were shelling out for that.

And I'd never forget that black mark warning his father had threatened me with.

But telling Nixon about it…what good would it do?

As much as I wanted to cling to Nixon and beg him to come up those stairs with me, I wouldn't do it.

I'd always love him. I'd always be his.

But I wouldn't be responsible for destroying the perfectly good life he'd carved out for himself.

When we were traveling back to LA together, I convinced myself that he was unhappy, that he needed me again to find his joy.

But I was wrong.

He'd made a life for himself. A good life.

I couldn't destroy it.

Stepping out of his embrace, I fought the belly-shaking tears by clearing my throat.

"I'm sorry I hurt you that summer. I'll always be sorry for that. But please believe me when I say that I only ever wanted you to be happy."

"You made me happy," he murmured.

"And so will she."

His forehead flickered with a frown.

"Come on, Nix, you know it's better this way. She's perfect. One look at her tells me she's from your world so she already fits. And if she even makes you the tiniest bit happy, you should go for it."

"Don't do this, please."

"Do what?"

"Make the choice for me."

"But that's what you need." I stepped forward and gripped his sweater. "You don't know what you want. Otherwise you would have been standing on my doorstep the night we got back to LA. She's a better fit than I will ever be."

Tears burned my eyes. I couldn't believe I was doing it again. Putting his happiness before mine. But what choice did I have?

Touching his face, I brushed my fingers down his cheek and smiled at him. "What we had in Yosemite was pure magic, but that's all it could ever be. Reality was waiting the second we got back to LA. And it was this time too. They'll be the best dreams I'll ever have. And they'll stay with me forever. But you need to go and live your life. The kind I can't have…or even offer you."

"But I love you," he whispered, his eyes glassing with tears. "I'll always love you."

It nearly broke me but I held fast, proving my point with a soft whisper. "Then go dump Shayna."

He grimaced, and I knew then that I was right.

Letting him go, I stepped back with a sad smile. "Your heart belongs to her now. Don't give it back to me. I'll only let you down and hurt you. After what I did, you can never fully trust me again. I'm a flight risk."

None of that was true. If I ever got him back, I'd cling with everything I had.

But he wasn't mine to cling to.

Reaching for my groceries, I held them against my chest and willed my body up those stairs.

Nixon stayed on the sidewalk, another sign that this was our last goodbye.

Pausing with a sigh, I turned and softly said, "Goodbye, Nixon. I honestly wish you all the happiness in the world. That's all I've ever wanted for you."

Before he could respond, I dashed up the stairs and unlocked the door, not looking back as I ducked inside and hid myself away.

The house was quiet, meaning Fliss and Maestro were out for a walk.

Pressing my forehead against the door, I slammed my teeth together as my entire body started shaking. The groceries slipped from my hand, crashing to the floor with a loud thump.

No one came rushing up to the stairs to check on me, which meant that Nixon had already walked away and was no doubt in his car driving home to his perfect future.

TWENTY-FIVE

NIXON

I drove away from Charlie's on autopilot. I didn't even know where I was going until my phone rang. I answered it without thinking.

"Hello." My voice was flat and emotionless.

"Hey, son. Where the hell are ya?" Dad's voice was bright yet demanding.

"Huh?" I frowned at the phone.

"Family dinner? You forget the plan? I got home from London this morning and we're all here waiting for ya."

"Oh." I sat up straighter behind the wheel, jolted by the reminder. "Yeah, of course, I just...totally blanked."

"Well, classes have started up again, so I guess that's understandable. But get your butt over here before everyone gets too tipsy on pre-dinner cocktails." He left me with a booming laugh and I turned right at the next intersection, heading for my parents' house.

It was a relief that he assumed classes were my issue. Like I could ever explain it to him. Charlie was right; they never really warmed to her. She wasn't a lady like my mother. I'd often wondered if she was just too much like Reagan. Like being around her was too painful and terrifying. The idea that their son could be led down the wrong path. When I first got back from Yosemite and told them our grand travel plans, I thought they were going to choke on their food. Charlie taking off like she had probably did them huge favors.

My parents would've hated her for dragging me overseas.

Shayna was the opposite. She loved family time. She brought all of us together. Even with the prospect of leaving for New York, she was scheduling trips so that we could stay in touch with both sets of parents. I was happy enough to go along with it. Family *was* important.

I swallowed, trying to legitimize Charlie's reasons for leaving.

Yeah, she probably would have pulled me from home a little, but we'd had every intention of coming back after we'd seen some of the world. It wasn't like she was trying to cut me off from them altogether.

But then when we got back…what would it have been like?

Awkward family dinners. My mother's jittery silence. Dad's cringe-worthy comments about her quirky fashion and lack of stability.

It would have been painful, hard work…

Worth it?

I didn't know.

Raking a hand through my hair, I turned left and took the slowest route to my parents' house. I needed time to collect my thoughts and pull myself together.

If I walked in the pale mess I felt, I'd be taken aside by all three of them and quietly asked if I was okay. I couldn't stomach it.

I didn't even remember making plans for the dinner, but I had vague recollections of Shayna telling me my dad was due back and we should get together to welcome him home.

Rubbing my eyes, I tried to shake Charlie from my mind and focus. Hopefully the dinner party was just my parents and Shayna. I had a sinking feeling it wouldn't be that easy. Nothing ever was.

Holding back a sigh, I turned up the volume on the radio and let music guide me home. "Gravity" by Against the Current rocked through the car and I had to wonder who would save me.

Charlie was a flight risk.

I felt like I was free-falling.

The only grounded person who knew exactly what she wanted was Shayna.

She made sense, yet my heart still kicked out of beat when I imagined marrying her.

I slowed the car and turned right, braking just before the gate. Punching in the number like I had a hundred times before, I turned the music down and refused to dwell on the sadness swirling in my stomach.

My world felt like it was shattering, but that was only because Charlie had come back into it. Before that it was stable. I knew the plan, could see the path.

I was happy.

Swallowing my doubts, I drove up the driveway and parked beside our Tudor-style home with its special blend of wood and stone. Mom had designed it years ago, no doubt basing it on her childhood fairy-tale fantasies.

Clearing my throat, I slid out of my car and spun the keys around my index finger as I walked. It was my little ritual when approaching my parents' home, like I had to psych myself up for whatever would hit me next.

Being the only child was a lot of pressure, and after their reaction to losing Reagan, I'd made it my mission to ease their pain. The best way to do that was to make them proud. The only time I'd swayed from my resolve was when I fell in love with Charlie. Man, I would have fought for her. If she'd just stuck around.

I still found it weird that she said she left for me.

Was I so blinded by love that I didn't see the writing on the wall?

How was it possible that she was able to look into the future before I did? I was the practical one; she was the dreamer. It was so unlike her to see the brewing storm and run from it.

With an irritated huff, I shook my head and stepped inside only to be met by my father.

"Son." He beckoned me down to his library. The look on his face was that of an excited kid.

My eyebrows furrowed as I glanced towards the living room.

To my disappointment, I could hear more than Shayna's and Mom's voices.

"Quick." Dad beckoned again and I picked up my pace, stepping into the room so he could close the door behind me.

He gave me an expectant look, so I raised my eyebrows and murmured, "Welcome home?"

Tipping his head back with a laugh, he slapped my shoulder and gave it a squeeze. His keen eyes looked me up and down before he chuckled again and pulled something from his jacket pocket. "I have a little something for you."

My insides jerked to a stop when I spotted the velvet blue ring box.

Shit. I'd forgotten all about the damn ring with its high and mighty history.

The box squeaked softly as Dad lifted the lid and showed me the pear-shaped diamond. It was kind of huge and would have totally engulfed Charlie's finger. It wasn't her style at all.

But I wasn't marrying Charlie.

The ring was perfect for Shayna, the band

covered in small diamonds. It was elegant, classy…everything she was.

With shaking fingers, I reached forward and lifted it out of the box.

"Wow," I croaked.

"I know. It's a beauty. And the story behind it is one of historic romance. It's beautiful. Exactly what Shayna wants."

"Yeah." I nodded.

My body was stiff for some reason, and I nearly dropped the ring as I tried to slot it back into the padded box.

"Careful, son." Dad steadied my hand, then chuckled. "I know you're nervous, but you have no reason to be. She's an amazing woman."

"Yeah." I swallowed. "Yeah, she is."

"Then why don't you look excited?" Dad's eyes narrowed.

A cold sweat broke out on the back of my neck as I licked my lips and lied. "How much did it cost?"

"Is that your concern?" Dad laughed again and gave my shoulder another squeeze. "Don't worry about paying me back. I've got you covered. Think of it as a gift from your mother and me."

I grimaced. "It's okay. I've got the money."

"You just leave it in that trust fund a little while longer. You're going to need all the help you can get when you move to New York. It's an expensive city and you'll have a wife with expensive tastes. Believe me, I know all about that." Dad's laughter grated on my nerves.

"You ever regret marrying Mom?" The question came out of frickin' nowhere and surprised us both.

His dark eyebrows popped high while I clamped my lips together, already dreading the response.

"Of course not. Where's this coming from?" Dad's voice dropped low with concern.

"Nowhere, I just…" My right shoulder hitched. "Marriage is a big deal."

"You getting cold feet?"

"Uh… No. I don't know." I shook my head and looked to the floor.

"Hey, listen to me for a second." Dad wrapped his arm around my shoulders. "Doubts are normal. It's okay to be a little nervous. There are plenty of girls in this world you could fall in love with. And plenty that would fall in love with you. But you have to use your head as well as your heart. Shayna's a good woman. You come from the same backgrounds, and you have so much in common. It's an easy match. Marriage can be hard sometimes, but if you marry someone with all the same values and aspirations, then half your battle's already won."

My mouth dried up as I listened to him.

"Everybody's expecting you to ask her, Nixon. That's why they're here."

My stomach bunched into a tight knot.

"You two make each other happy. This match makes sense. Your mother has been delirious since you two got together."

My head bobbed, but my throat was too thick to speak.

"I remember questioning myself before I proposed to your mother. Was I making the right choice? What if there was someone better out there that I hadn't met yet? But you know, you can't think that way. Choose Shayna now, and I guarantee you won't regret it. Being with her will make for a smooth sail." Dad pulled away and gave me a bright grin. "So, unless you can give me a perfectly good reason not to marry her…"

I went still and thought about Charlie. She flittered through my mind, a rainbow feather that had enchanted me and then left me empty when she floated away on the breeze.

"Nixon?" Worry deepened the wrinkles around Dad's eyes, his joke giving way to anxious surprise. "Do you have a good reason?"

"No," I finally croaked. "No, I don't have a good reason."

It was the truth. Shayna was all the things Dad said she was, and I didn't have a good reason not to marry her.

Because Charlie wasn't a good reason.

She was an unreliable reason based solely on heart.

"Alright then," Dad murmured. "Well, why don't you get on out there and make your mother and me proud?"

I swallowed, my head bobbing like my neck was made of silly string.

"Son." Dad paused with his hand on the door

knob. "This family has been through a lot of pain with losing Reagan and…all." He cast his eyes to the floor. "But the last two years have been a real ray of sunshine for us. I can't express how much it means to feel this kind of joy again."

How the hell did I rebut that?

Forcing a smile, I nodded at him to open the door, then made my way down to the living room.

My shoes echoed on the polished wood, sounding ominous as I approached.

The second Mom spotted me, she let out a delighted greeting and soon every eye in the room was zeroed in on me.

I focused on Shayna and willed myself to walk toward her.

She smiled at me, sweet and excited, already knowing what was coming.

Pushing down the ravenous nerves, I walked around the couch and found a place beside her. Glancing at her parents and extended family, I gave them a shy smile before looking at Dad. He nodded, then winked. And I did the only thing I could.

Hitching my pant leg, I dropped to one knee and set a stable course for my future.

No rainbows.

No trips around the world.

But security with a beautiful woman who loved me and would always be my gravity.

TWENTY-SIX

CHARLIE

I spent the night crying in my room. I heard Fliss and Maestro come home but pretended to be asleep when she popped her head in to check on me. She snuck out with a soft apology, and I clung to my pillow to muffle the tears.

By the time I got up at nine o'clock to take a shower, I was shattered.

I just wanted to soak in a hot spray before officially going to bed.

I was a worn-out, tattered mess, my head pounding while my heart disintegrated. I hadn't cried so much since I'd left Nixon four years ago.

Aunt Jessica wasn't there to mop up my tears either.

It was tempting to go to Mom. She'd hug me, but then she'd also swaddle me in advice that would be more a pep talk than anything. I couldn't stomach it.

I could just head back to Montana. There was a certain sense of solace there.

But then what?

After a few months I'd get bored and need to move again. I couldn't keep spending my life jumping from Montana to LA to Seattle to Portland, then down to San Diego. I couldn't keep doing that. All the different jobs, the constant sense of restlessness.

The wedding photography gig had been my steadiest income and I kept coming back to it. But the thought of doing that, like actually enduring another wedding, kind of nauseated me. It was fine when there was still a chance of true love for me. I could snap photos of the couples kissing and committing their lives to each other, secretly hoping that one day I'd be that bride, kissing Nixon.

My wedding wouldn't be white and traditional.

I'd come up with all sorts of colorful, wacky scenarios.

But I couldn't waste my time doing that anymore.

That chance was over. My hope was gone.

I needed something to channel my focus, bring me out of the depressing vortex.

I needed clarity.

Switching off the shower, I quickly dried myself and decided to chat with Fliss. She always made me talk until I could think clearly. She was so wasted on animals. She should seriously be studying psychology, not doing veterinary training.

"We need wine, chocolates and a good chat." I flicked off the bathroom fan and heard a soft moan coming from the living room.

My nose wrinkled, and then I rolled my eyes.

"That better be a frickin' movie," I muttered, tying back my hair as I stomped down the hallway.

But no. Lucky me. It was a live-action romance featuring my roommate and her rock star boyfriend.

Fliss was on Flick's knee, mewling as his hands gripped her ass and they got busy with a heated make-out session.

Jealousy ripped through me like a green monster, and it took everything in me not to throw the TV remote at their heads.

"If you guys do it on the couch again, I'm seriously burning that thing!"

They jumped apart. Fliss yelped and laughed as she reclasped her bra, then straightened her shirt. Flick's eyes were hot with desire when he winked at her.

She giggled and turned to face me.

Maestro scampered across the wooden floor and I crouched down to give him a quick pet while glaring at my roommate.

Her smile was near blinding as she skipped over to me. I stood, preparing myself for the worst. Fliss only got super giggly when the news was epic.

"You're not going to believe it." She stole a glance at Flick who grinned at her. She giggled and held up a trembling hand. "I'm engaged!"

The only response I could manage was a little squeak as I took her hand and gaped at the ring.

It was a simple diamond…a freaking huge simple diamond, but still nothing fancy. The rock was set inside a band of white gold. Stunning yet subtle. So incredibly Fliss.

Flick snickered as he rearranged the beanie on his head. "I know. The last thing you expected, right?"

I looked at him, still struggling to form a sentence.

"Truth is, I was just going to ask her to move in with me, but then I figured if we were going to be living together, we may as well be engaged, you know?"

"So freaking traditional. The last thing I expected from you, baby." Fliss shook her head, staring at the ring in wonder.

Flick smiled at her, the gooey kind that makes girls swoon, and whispered, "Complex, sweetness."

She rolled her eyes and giggled again.

"Wow." I finally breathed, then forced myself to choke out the best congratulations I could. "I'm so happy for you guys."

I was. It didn't seem like it in that particular

moment, but I seriously was. Fliss and Flick may have been on and off again, but they always came back together. They were made for each other, even in those moments when they didn't want to be.

It was good that Flick acknowledged that. I was happy for Fliss.

It was great.

I was…happy.

Fliss gave me a pained smile. "I know this is kind of springing the whole moving out thing on you, but I'm not actually planning on leaving until the summer starts. I'm so close to classes here, so it makes sense to move after they've finished."

"Of course." I nodded.

"You're not…upset, are you? I can help you find a new roommate."

"No." I brushed my hand through the air. "I'm not even sure what I'll be doing this summer, so the timing could be perfect for us to let go of this place."

"Oh, okay." Fliss's pale eyebrows rose. "Do you have a plan?"

"Not yet." I winked, making her laugh. She was too euphoric to notice how forced I was being, and that kind of suited me. It wasn't the time to shit all over her happy parade with my depressive wanderings.

Squeezing Fliss's hand, I forced my brightest smile. "Seriously, it's so awesome. I'm so happy for you guys."

They grinned at each other and I could feel the vibe electrifying between them. They'd be having sex soon, and I didn't want to be around to hear it.

I was about to step back towards the door when Flick said, "Let's get going, sweetness. The guys are all waiting at the house to celebrate."

Fliss let out this girly squeal and sprinted to her room. "I'll just grab my stuff."

"You want to come, Chuck?" Flick pulled the keys from his pocket.

I shook my head. "No, I've got a…"

His eyes narrowed at the corners, reading me in ways I didn't want him to.

"I am seriously happy for you guys."

"That's the third time you've said that in about five minutes."

Damn his keen eyes and intelligence!

"But I am. I swear." I licked my lips when his scrutiny didn't let up. "I'm just…uh… I'm having my own personal crisis right now and before you ask me if I'm okay, please don't. I'm not ready to talk about it."

He pursed his lips and nodded. "I get it. But whatever the hell it is, don't let it eat you alive. You beat that bitch with music or action or whatever you need to do." He tipped his head toward the hallway. "You know Fliss will listen to anything you have to say, right?"

I gave him a closed-mouth smile. "Yeah. But not on the night she gets engaged, okay?"

He snickered and raised his eyebrows with a nod. "Look, I know it's a big deal to lose her. You guys have had fun here. But just because she's moving in with me doesn't mean she won't be there for you."

"I know," I whispered before shuffling away from his penetrating gaze.

He thought I was gutted because I was losing my roommate. And for sure, I was. I loved living with Fliss. But that wasn't what was killing me.

As I stepped into my room and leaned against the back of my door, the thing that made my knees buckle was the truth that all the people I loved were moving on.

And I was stagnant.

Stuck in this holding pattern.

Waiting for something that was never going to happen.

My stomach jerked with a sob, but I wouldn't set it free. I'd cried enough to last me the next two decades.

I slammed my teeth together and wiped my finger under my nose.

I had no idea how long I sat on my floor doing that. Fliss called out a goodbye. The front door shut behind her. Maestro's nails clicked on the floor. He sniffed around my door for me, and when I didn't respond he disappeared, no doubt to his squishy bed in the living room.

My butt was sore and aching by the time I finally moved. Crawling over to my computer, I opened Spotify and scanned the playlist, looking for something to get me out of my funk.

Music had magical qualities and damn, did I need some magic in that moment.

Pushing my finger up the mouse pad, the list of

songs in my extensive playlist turned to white fuzz.

I couldn't even find music to listen to.

Squeezing my eyes shut, I bashed my finger onto the pad with a yell.

And soft piano music started up.

I recognized the tune within eight beats—"Carry On" by Fun.

Sitting motionless on my knees, I stared at the screen until it became a blur. The lyrics spun around me, sinking in and speaking to me the way music always had in the past.

The sad voice understood me and I gazed up at the ceiling, fighting tears.

"If you're lost and alone…," he sang.

I closed my eyes, tears trickling down my cheeks as I soaked in the chorus.

Then the drumbeat kicked in and I knew…

I knew what I had to do.

Move forward.

Move on.

Let go of a pipe dream.

I'd walked away for Nixon's sake. Because I was trying to do the right thing.

But deep down, I hadn't left him at all.

It was time to do it for real.

Jerking up, I grabbed my chair and sat down, then pulled up a new tab in my browser. As the song built around me, my fingers flew over the keys. I started with a dream, just Googling pictures of places in the world to inspire me. And then it turned to research, which became a scrawled plan on paper. As the clock ticked past two, I'd worked out how much money I still needed to save to see the places I'd dreamed of for years. My beautiful plan had taken shape and inspired something inside of me.

With my finger hovering over the pad, I stared at the PURCHASE TICKET button and whispered, "Carry on," before taking the plunge and securing a one-way flight out of LAX.

3 MONTHS LATER

TWENTY-SEVEN

CHARLIE

I'd been working my ass off, saving like a fiend and taking every spare job I could find, from family photos to graduation pics and a ton of weddings.

In less than three weeks I'd be boarding a plane to my new life. I headed towards it with a mixture of excitement and terror.

My first stop was Hawaii, where I'd already booked one week at a hostel. It was kind of scary heading off on my own, but determination would push me through. I had to get away. I couldn't be on the same continent when Nixon slipped a wedding ring on someone else's finger.

"So, you seem really set on this." Fliss sucked her Jamba Juice straw, her eyes kind of sad as she walked beside me down the street.

"I've already paid for the tickets, Flissy. I have to go."

Pausing outside an outdoor and travel store, I gave her a brave smile before pushing the door open. We strolled in together and the first thing to hit me was the smell—that mixture of new canvas and plastic utensils, intelligent knickknacks that compacted everyday living down to travel size.

Basically, it smelled like adventure.

People who shopped in places like this had plans, big plans, based on dreams of seeing the world in a way that others never would.

Fliss and I scanned the store for packs.

"Over there." She pointed.

My lips stretched into a wide smile as I headed for the wall of brightly colored backpacks. I wanted something slimline and easy to carry, yet big enough to hold all my stuff. It meant I would scream tourist wherever I went, which wasn't exactly preferable, but I had to be practical as well.

I took a bright orange pack off the hook. "This one's kind of cool." I started unzipping compartments and checking out all the little places I could hide my passport and important stuff. "This'll be big enough, right?"

"It depends how long you're going for." Fliss's tone was dry, taking us right back to the argument we'd been having ever since I told her my plans.

"Would you let that go already? I've set money

aside so I can come home as soon as I'm done."

"Yes, but when is that? Two months? A year? Two years?"

I huffed, the pack hitting my knees as my arms went straight. "I don't know, okay? As long as it takes."

"He's going to be married for the rest of his life, Chuck. And you can't stay away forever."

Some days I wished I hadn't told her a damn thing about Nixon, but she wouldn't let me get away with "It's just time to go." So we'd stayed up until four in the morning one night and I told her the whole wretched story.

"You should have told his dad to stick it! I can't believe he showed up at your door like that!"

"They were right though. I can't give him a stable, nine-to-five life. That would have killed me…and driven us apart."

Fliss had huffed, trying to convince me that maybe he didn't want that for himself. But I knew better. He wouldn't be getting married if he didn't want the security of a normal life. He wouldn't drive a wedge between himself and his only family. His parents needed him. And he knew it. He was too good a person to let them down.

I pulled the pack on, settling it over my shoulders and clipping the waist belt. "This feels good."

Fliss gave me a defeated smile.

"Would you stop? I need you to be happy for me."

"I would be if I wasn't so worried. Are you sure

about going alone?"

"I'll be fine! It's what I want."

"No, it's not. But I guess it is what it is." Fliss shrugged and slurped some more of her juice.

"I'm sorry I'm going to miss your wedding," I whispered, wondering if that was really the root cause of her major reluctance over me leaving.

"It's not that. We haven't even set a date yet. And in fairness to you, I'm moving out and leaving you all alone, so really, your timing is impeccable."

My nose started to tingle as I stared at Fliss—my cousin-in-law turned close friend. We'd been rooming together for a while, and it'd been awesome.

I was going to miss her big time.

In a lame attempt to make her smile, I grabbed her hand and gave it a little squeeze…then started singing "Cups."

Fliss's lips twitched, and once again proving how awesome she was, she kicked in with a harmony. We stood in the store singing loud enough to turn heads. But we didn't care.

It was a beautiful moment that would be burned into my memory…and would no doubt carry me along on those moments away from home, when I felt the weight of my solitary life.

TWENTY-EIGHT

NIXON

It'd been three long months, only made worse by the fact that in a few short weeks my fate would be sealed. After proposing to Shayna, I'd expected everything to magically fall into place. Like my brain would understand that I'd made my choice and my feelings for Charlie would quickly die off as I looked ahead to the future.

But it hadn't worked.

I still dreamed about her, found my mind floating toward her whenever I lost focus for a moment.

As a way to counter my unrest, I'd thrown

myself into school and studying.

But as I walked up the front steps, carrying my graduation robe, I had to face the truth. Study time was over…and my life was about to change for good.

Dread simmered inside me and I had to ask myself yet again why the hell I was going through with it. I hadn't been able to answer the question with any kind of clarity so I just kept riding the wave, keeping everybody happy so I didn't break hearts.

I was able to process my feelings in my journal. Yeah, it made me sound like a teenage girl, but I'd always been a writer and being able to pen my woes somehow helped. Traveling across the country with Charlie had reminded me of the long-buried passion, and each night after Shayna fell asleep, I'd pull out my diary and write a few pages. It was good to process it all—it helped me line up my logic and reminded me why going with the flow was the right thing to do.

I couldn't break Shayna's heart now. The ring was on her finger, the wedding mere weeks away. We'd come too far, and somehow I had to make it work.

Opening the door with a heavy sigh, I hung up my robe in the hallway closet and headed down to my room.

Music was playing in our bedroom, and as I walked down the hall, the words hit me with a brutal poignancy.

"I don't want to feel like this tomorrow."

I stopped walking and slid my hands into my pockets, soaking in the rest of the words to "Never Surrender" by Skillet.

It was supposed to be a love song. Surrendering to the woman you wanted to be with. But it was working completely differently for me. It was hammering home the fact that I didn't want to be caught in this trap anymore. I didn't want to trudge through life fighting to secure my happiness. I wanted to surrender. To be myself.

I wanted to feel actual joy without having to convince myself to do it.

And the only person I'd ever been able to do that around was Charlie.

Squeezing my burning eyes shut, I muttered, "Why the fuck did you leave me?"

I knew.

She'd told me. And I got why she did, even though she said she didn't really want to.

It didn't take away the pain and the hurt, but…

My eyes popped open.

But I never chased her.

I never fought.

I bought into my parents' reasoning about how wild and unreliable Charlie was. I made myself believe that I was too plain and boring for her. I bought into it all as a way to understand, but the truth was still there, plain and simple…

Charlie Watson made me a happy man.

When I looked back on my life, the times I felt most alive were when I was with her.

So why the hell was I marrying Shayna?

Scrubbing a hand down my face, I headed for my bedroom and stopped in the doorway.

My fiancée was sitting on my side of the bed, going through my bedside cabinet. Books and my journal were laid out on the mattress, and my gut spiked with fear.

Shit! Had she read the journal?

I'd put everything in there…including the fact that I'd nearly slept with Charlie on my road trip. If Shayna read that she'd be crushed.

And that was when it hit me…revelation number two.

I was a selfish asshole.

A coward who was allowing Shayna to surge ahead with wedding plans and setting up our future when I wasn't even into it. I'd been so wrong, thinking that I was somehow saving her pain.

But letting this happen was incredibly unfair.

Was I honestly expecting her to spend the rest of her life with a husband who didn't love her with his whole heart?

It was time to man-up before she figured out that I couldn't give her what she needed.

I cleared my throat, trying to counter the dread that was blocking my windpipe.

Shayna glanced up and smiled at me. "You get your robe?"

I nodded. "What…what are you doing?"

"I'm just getting the whole packing thing started. I figured I'd do some major culling first. I've thrown out two boxes of my stuff already, and

I'm now moving on to yours." She ran her hands over the stack of old books. "Do you know you've kept like every book from high school?"

That wasn't true. I'd only kept the ones that had notes and doodles from Charlie in the margins.

"Biology, English, World History. Why are you keeping these? It's not like you'll ever refer to them again."

I stepped into the room. "They're memories, Shayna. That's not the kind of stuff you cull."

She rolled her eyes. "Your mother warned me you'd be like this."

"Like what?"

"Clinging to the past." Her smile softened with sympathy. "Don't worry, I won't throw away anything to do with Reagan."

My mouth went dry. I hadn't even thought about my late sister. She had nothing to do with my precious memories from high school.

"So, I was thinking maybe you could keep your journal and some yearbooks. But school stuff? As in notes you took in class…maybe not so much." She cringed like I was a loser and laughed. "Besides, baby, we can't fit this into a New York apartment. You either have to throw it out or store stuff at your parents'. It's just reality."

"But I don't want it to be my reality," I muttered.

"Excuse me?" Shayna's frown was marked and quickly turning into the one I did everything to avoid.

But it was time to stop dodging conflict and face

it head-on.

Pressing my lips together, I sucked in a breath through my nose and sighed. "I don't want this."

"O-kay." She looked puzzled for a second and then started stacking up the books. "Fine. Keep them, but we'll have to sacrifice something else. I've been looking into apartments in New York and even though our parents are helping us out, we'll still be living in a shoebox. So, what are we going to sacrifice?"

All I could do was stare at her. She was beautiful with her sleek blonde hair and vibrant eyes. Her sharp, take-charge manner had pulled me out of a pit. But I couldn't keep owing her anymore.

It wasn't fair to either of us.

"Hello? Nixon!" She waved her hand in the air to grab my attention. "I can't do this on my own, okay? I know you've been really busy with your studies and I've been in charge of *everything* else, which is fine, but I need you to focus now. We have a life to plan."

"I know. Always a plan, right?" I snickered and shook my head. "From the day I was born, my whole life has been sketched out for me, carefully plotted and calculated so that I could have a safe, happy existence."

Shayna's eyes narrowed, her head jerking back like I was acting crazy. "Nixon, we've talked about this. We'll live in New York until you graduate law school and then—"

"I don't want to go to New York with you," I blurted, then let out this relieved kind of laugh.

There, I'd said it. I'd finally fucking said it.

Running her finger down the delicate gold chain around her neck, she started playing with the heart pendant. Her eyes were still narrowed, her forehead wrinkled in confusion. "I don't understand."

I raked a hand through my hair and closed my eyes with a sigh. "I'm sorry, okay? I just went along with all of this because that's what everyone wanted me to do."

"Wow, okay." Shayna stood, and straightened her skirt before walking across the room to me. She was so much shorter without her heels on. If I tucked her against me, her forehead would nestle into the crook of my neck. I'd never feel that again after this conversation, and it was a sad kind of loss.

My throat was thick as Shayna rested her hand on my chest. I swallowed when she gently pinched my chin to make me look at her.

It was painful gazing into her eyes, but I made myself do it, because I couldn't be a coward anymore.

"Well, where do you want to go, then?" She smiled.

I winced, hating that she didn't get it. That I'd have to spell it out for her. "I need some time to figure out…what I want." Stepping back, I took her hands and rubbed my thumb over the ridiculous ring Dad had brought back from Europe. My face bunched with remorse. "I know how much you want New York. And I never wanted to let you down. I wanted to be the man you deserve."

"You are." She touched my cheek but I leaned away from her.

"I'm not, Shay." Letting her go, I put another foot between us and fought for the right words. "You deserve a guy who's going to give you his whole heart. Who's passionate about being with you and sharing the kind of life you want. I…I can't do that."

It was starting to dawn on her that I was launching into a break-up speech. The skin on her neck turned a mottled pink as she pressed her hand into her stomach.

"This isn't happening," she whispered.

Hating myself, I plowed on, needing to get it over and done with. "My heart belongs somewhere else. It always has, and I've tried so hard to move past it but I just… I can't."

She stumbled back from me and plonked onto the edge of the bed. Her eyes were round and unseeing as her chest heaved.

I crouched down beside her, gently resting my hand on her knee to try to somehow soften the blow. "It's unfair to marry you, Shayna. I'm so sorry I let it go this far. I thought I could be happy. I thought…"

Sucking in a ragged breath, she pushed my hand off her knee and swiveled away from me.

"I'm sorry," I whispered. "I don't want to hurt you."

Her fingers trembled as she threaded them together then gripped tight. She was blinking at the wall, her lips pinched into a thin line while she fought whatever emotions were trying to take her down.

I reached for her hands, desperate to make it better, but she jerked away from my touch.

"I'd rather you tell me now than the night before the wedding." Her voice shook. She pressed her hand against her forehead. "Although it is only sixteen days away." With a little whimper, she surged for the tissue box beside my bed.

Pulling out three, she bunched them against her eyes.

"I'm sorry." I said it again, desperate to make it right without capitulating. I was in it now. I had to see it through.

She cried for a few painful minutes while I crouched beside the bed. My mind kept playing tricks on me, warning me of the repercussions of my actions.

I nearly folded. But I'd come this far; I couldn't back out.

Finally Shayna glanced over her shoulder and sniffed. "Did you ever love me?"

"Of course I love you." I sat on the bed beside her, running my hand down her back. "I just don't love you enough to deserve you."

She scoffed and shuffled away from my touch. "I hate bullshit lines like that."

"I'm just trying to be honest. Which is really hard for me. I hate letting people down and I have seriously been trying so hard. But I can't. I can't be the husband you deserve. You are an amazing, wonderful woman and should be with a man who only wants to be with you. Someone who enjoys all the things in life that you enjoy."

Her lips flatlined, her eyes narrowing into a heated glare. My speech was obviously doing nothing to comfort her, even though I meant every word of it.

"Who is she?" Her voice was sharp and metallic.

I hesitated until Shayna huffed.

"Don't tell me I can't have your whole heart and then *not* tell me who it belongs to!"

I swallowed and scratched the side of my neck. "A girl I went to high school with."

"Charlie?" Her voice pitched high. "That summer fling?"

I stiffened and couldn't help a confused frown. "H-how do you know about Charlie?"

She scoffed and slashed a tear off her cheek. "Your dad told me all about it. She was some reckless girl who wanted to pull you away from your family. Your mother was so upset, but you were so blinded by her influence."

"That's...that's not true, actually."

"Whatever. She was destroying your family, okay? If your dad hadn't intervened, she—"

"What?" I cut her off.

Shayna frowned at my interruption. "They knew she was going to break your heart, so he stepped in to save you guys and keep the family together. And she did exactly what he thought she would. She just took off without a word, breaking your heart." She waved her hand in the air then slapped it down on her knee. "That's the girl you'd rather be with?"

"Protect me?" I shot off the bed and spun to face her. "What did he do? Did he say something to her?"

Her right eyebrow arched, but then she averted her gaze to the floor. "I don't know all the details. He just told me that she was leading you astray and he had a quiet word with her to make sure she wasn't going to ruin your life. But then she did. She just left! And that's why he's so grateful to me, and why he's so happy we're together. Because he knows I would never do something like that to you."

My heart pounded, my head reeling as I tried to take in what she was saying.

Dad had intervened.

Anger bubbled. No wonder she took off.

He convinced her she wasn't good enough for me!

And then Mom sold me on the fact that Charlie was some impulsive, flighty chick who wasn't right for me.

Did she know about Dad's *quiet word?*

I squeezed my head, breathing hard as I tried to rein in the heated emotions.

"Do you even know where she is?" Shayna spat. "You haven't seen her in like four years. Unless you've secretly been having an affair with her this whole time."

"No." I shook my head, distracted.

"So, why now? Why on the brink of our

wedding is this all coming to a head? You're going to hurt a lot of people with this decision."

"I know," I croaked, finally looking her in the eye. "But all this time I've been ignoring the problem because I didn't want to hurt you. I thought if I just tried hard enough, I could…" My shoulders deflated with a sigh. "I know I've said this already, but you need to marry a guy who can give you all the things you want. Someone who'll be devoted and adoring. Someone you can be yourself around."

"I *am* myself around you."

"But I'm not me around you." I sighed. "I can never fully relax because I'm always worried I'll do something you don't like. I go with the flow because it's peaceful and easy, and you like it that way. But it's not what I want."

She gave me an incredulous look. I'd apparently hidden things pretty damn well, because my big confession was obviously coming out of left field. Her jaw worked to the side as she shook her head. She was clearly annoyed that I'd been living a lie this whole time.

"What…what do you want, then?"

"I want Charlie," I whispered. "I want to be with Charlie."

Shayna's expression crumpled. Tears built on her lashes and quickly slid free.

I brushed them away with my thumb. "How do I make this better?"

She sniffed and pulled herself straight, gently flicking my hand away from her. "You leave. You take your stuff and you walk out that door. And don't even think about contacting me again."

Her voice was soft yet commanding. I almost felt wounded, but I knew survival mode when I saw it.

"I need the clean break." She raised her chin. "I can't drag this out and torture myself with the idea that maybe you'll change your mind. Even if you do, I don't want you back. This is it for us, so just go. The faster the better."

Her hard line was pure defense. So Shayna. She'd never been one to mess around.

I swallowed the lump in my throat and asked in a husky voice, "Are you going to be okay?"

"Harper will be home soon. We'll get drunk and curse your name." Her glare was a mixture of pain and mourning.

I stood and moved away from it, opening my mouth to apologize again.

"Don't." She shook her head. "It'd be so much worse if you were saying this in five years."

Dipping her head, she stood and walked out of the room.

The front door slammed shut behind her, and I was left alone to pack my stuff and leave.

TWENTY-NINE

CHARLIE

"So you're all packed?" Mom passed me a cup of peach iced tea and took a seat beside me.

We were in her cluttered little kitchen, at the round wooden table that had been sitting in the corner ever since they'd moved in five years ago.

Five years. That was a record for them.

Mom and Dad had saved for years to be able to afford their own place. We'd jumped from one rental property to another, until *finally* in my senior year of high school, they'd found this place and had enough deposit to secure it. They'd be paying off the mortgage for at least another twenty years, but they owned a tiny slice of LA, and they couldn't be more house-proud if they tried.

Dad was out in the garden, singing off-key while he weeded and pruned. It'd taken Mom all of five minutes to roll her eyes and turn the radio on.

"Comeback Kid" by Against the Current was keeping us company as I answered Mom's question.

"I've got everything organized. The apartment needs cleaning, but I'll meet Fliss there this afternoon to do that. And then we hand over the keys."

"I bet she's excited." Mom wiggled her eyebrows.

I laughed and shook my head. "She'll go crazy living in that Chaos zoo with everyone, but she's in love." I shrugged. "And you do crazy stuff when you're in love."

Mom gave me a meaningful smile and patted my hand. "Well, I'm glad you're here for a few nights before leaving. It's nice to spend some time with my girl."

Emotion rose up and choked me. All I could do was blink and fight the tears.

My ever perceptive mother gave me a wink and changed the subject.

"So, you all set for the wedding on Saturday?"

"Uh-huh." I swallowed and rubbed my eyes. "My last one. It feels weird. I've been doing so many lately."

"You've been working yourself to the bone. I'm glad it's coming to an end. It's high time you started doing what you've been wanting to all along."

"Yeah, well, I probably should have done it a couple of years ago." I sipped my tea. The icy sweetness was delicious, the perfect partner on a hot day.

"You had to save your pennies first." Mom's salt-and-pepper curls shook as she nodded.

I tipped my head back and looked to the ceiling. "Aw, come on, we both know it was fear that held me back."

"And hope." Mom's hand was back on top of mine, giving it a little rub and forcing more tears to pop onto my lashes.

My jaw trembled. "Fruitless hope. Just because I never moved on or slept with anybody else didn't mean he wouldn't. I can't believe I expected it to be the same for him. I hurt him. I don't deserve him, Mom."

She disagreed with me on that point, but we'd argued enough and she knew better than to try again. Although my parents didn't really want me with someone whose family would cause me stress, they *did* want me to be happy. When I told Mom about my road trip and confessed all my long-buried hope, she'd held me while I cried and maybe changed her tune on the whole me and Nixon thing.

Maybe if she'd realized just how much I'd loved him back in high school she wouldn't have encouraged me to move to Montana.

But I couldn't change the past…and neither

could she.

Running her finger around the lip of her glass, she spoke softly, like I was five years old and she was coaxing me to my first day of school. "Sometimes we make mistakes and we can't fix them. No one's ever said life would be fair. But when something is meant to be, it does have an amazing way of working out. Look at Troy and Cassie. They got engaged years ago and one thing after another has held up the wedding."

I let out a soft snort. It was true. First there was Felix's skateboard accident. Two broken wrists, surgery, and months of recovery. The wedding was postponed until he was able to play guitar again. He was set on performing at their wedding, and they were happy to wait.

But then attempt number two was thwarted by that massive storm that flooded the wedding venue two days before the big event. Cassie figured it must be a sign and canceled everything. Troy wouldn't let her back out completely and tried to convince her to get married in a courthouse. Apparently Felix went nuts, saying his aunt deserved the most beautiful wedding in the world. And so they were attempting a third time. They'd pulled out all the stops for this one. Everybody was praying and crossing their fingers that this would be it.

"Saturday is going to be a perfect day, because they've overcome the odds and stuck it out. They're meant to be together."

I gave my mom a watery smile. "So, who I am

meant to be with, then?"

"I wish I could tell you." Mom's eyes gleamed along with mine. Blinking, she sniffed and sat up, resting her elbows on the table and leaning toward me with a confident smile. "I don't know if it's Nixon or not, but one thing I do know is that you have wanted to travel the world since you were a tiny tot. You were always dreaming about seeing every color and every country. That's what you're meant to be doing. And on Sunday, you will. You'll fly, and you'll find yourself all over again. This is going to be the making of you."

"I just wish I wasn't going alone." I finally admitted the truth.

"But you're strong enough to go alone. You can handle it, Charlotte."

My nose wrinkled at the use of my full name.

Mom laughed and shook her head. "I would have put Charlie on the birth certificate if your father would have let me. From the second I laid eyes on you, I knew you were going to be different from all the other girls out there. You're like a rainbow, and you've made our lives brilliant. You're going to light up the lives of everyone you come in contact with. Make that your goal, sweet girl. You go light up the world."

THIRTY

NIXON

I drove to my parents' house in agitated silence. My fingers tapped the wheel as I sped around a corner and onto the next road.

Part of me was still livid that Dad had 'intervened' and ruined my chances with Charlie. But another part was scared to tell them that I'd finally found my balls and was ready to fight for the girl I'd wanted all along.

They were going to go apeshit.

And their apeshit was scarier than my wrath. I knew that already.

Shit, everyone was going to go crazy when they

heard what I'd done.

I dumped Shayna.

From the outside, me walking away from that gorgeous, lovable girl was certifiably insane.

And maybe I was a little crazy.

But I'd go out of mind if I entered the life everyone was planning for me.

If I didn't break free, I'd spend the rest of my pathetic years wondering.

The back of my mind warned me that I could be making a massive mistake. But something in my chest told me to keep fighting.

I braked and punched in the gate code. The gate ground open and I zoomed in the second it was wide enough. My nerves pulsated like a freaking strobe light as I pulled up beside the house.

Shutting off the engine, I gripped the wheel for a minute, clenching my jaw and willing my anger not to fade. I needed it to get me through.

A slice of fear sizzled through me, the impending battle nearly making me back out.

"Stop being so fucking pathetic," I whispered as I hitched my jeans and walked to the door.

Twenty-two years old and still afraid to defy my parents. It was ridiculous.

Thoughts of Reagan tortured me when I reached the door.

"Leave me alone," I gritted between clenched teeth.

It wasn't fair. I couldn't live on a guilt trip anymore.

My shoes echoed on the polished floor as I

walked into the house. "Hey, Mom and Dad. It's me," I called into the cavernous entrance.

Memories of the first time I'd brought Charlie over suddenly assaulted me. She'd looked so small in the big entrance, her vibrant color slightly dimmed by the austere surroundings. Then my mother had walked in, adding another shade of gray as she so eloquently demeaned my precious friend. Charlie had been wearing bright red shoes, yellow shorts and a shirt that looked like a paint pallet had thrown up on it. I loved that shirt.

Mom? Not so much.

She'd cast her eyes down Charlie's body like the girl had mental problems.

The woman had never understood the unique rainbow that Charlie was. It'd always been lost on her.

Charlie had stood up to my mother's cold reception with her spunky flair, but the politely veiled insults had obviously eaten at her more than she let on.

My shoulders tensed with anger. I still couldn't stomach the fact that Charlie had been cornered by my dad, no doubt fed a nasty diatribe about how unworthy she was, and then believed it.

She'd believed it.

The thought made me sick.

I should have gone after her. I should have driven to Montana and begged her to reconsider, convinced her that we could overcome the odds together.

"Nixon." Mom's delighted greeting was

punctured by her heels on the floor. Even on a Friday evening in, she was still dressed up like she was going out. The woman was all class and elegance. She felt most comfortable when she looked great, and probably didn't even understand the beauty of sweatpants or the awesomeness of ripped jeans and a sloppy, oversized T-shirt.

"What are you doing here?" She smiled. "Are you all set for graduation?"

"Yeah. My robe's in the car."

"Wonderful. I can't wait." She kissed my cheek and gave me a hug. "My amazing boy. I'm so proud. I don't know what I'd do without you."

My smile was tight as I gazed down at her.

"So, what can we do for you? Or are you just here to visit?" Her eyes were dancing, bright with hope and expectation. First my engagement, then my acceptance to Columbia. The next day I'd be graduating, and then I was getting married and moving to New York to eventually become a high-flying lawyer. My mother was going for the triple win—everything she wanted.

Shit. She'll take losing the wedding hard.

But I couldn't keep up the facade anymore.

And maybe she deserved a little hurt after everything she'd inflicted on me. Scheming behind my back. Manipulating me.

Anger made my jaw clench.

Oblivious, Mom flicked her hand and led me into the library. A glass of malt whiskey was next to Dad's red armchair while a bulbous glass of merlot was beside the couch next to Mom's open book.

"I don't know where your father's disappeared to, but I'm sure he'll be back in a second."

Tucking her skirt beneath her legs, she sat down on the couch and crossed her ankles before smiling up at me.

"Can I get you a drink, sweetheart?"

"No, I'm good." Sliding my hands into my pockets, I gazed down at the cream rug and fought a wave of nausea.

"Well, take a seat. Tell me about your day."

I had to get it over with. Pressing my lips together, I counted to three and then blurted, "Shayna and I broke up."

My voice was quiet but the words still exploded into the room, shocking the hell out of my mother.

She blinked, then laughed and shook her head. "I'm sorry. I don't think I heard you correctly because you just said you and Shayna broke up, and that can't be right."

"Why? Because it doesn't fit into your plan for me?" I looked her in the eye, my tone sharp and defiant.

Her head jerked back like I'd just slapped her. "Where is this coming from?"

"I'm sorry, Mom, but I can't do this anymore. I'm my own man. I officially resign from beneath your care…and manipulation."

My words were spiky and hard, but she acted like they were balls of cotton wool.

Running her finger down her sleek hairline, she fought for control with a polite smile, then brushed her hand through the air. "It's okay, we can sort this out. Let me call Shayna's mother. We'll get you two together, have some mediation. It'll be fine. Let me get my phone." Standing tall, she brushed past me and out the door just as Dad stepped into the room.

He grinned at me, his eyes lighting the way they always did. "Hey, son."

I ignored him and called into the hallway. "I don't want you to sort it out, Mom."

"Yes you do, honey. It'll be okay."

"No! Get back in here!" I shouted.

Dad's frown was sharp, distorting his long handsome face. "What are you thinking talking to your mother that way? What's going on?"

I sighed and admitted in a heavy voice, "I broke up with Shayna."

"*You* broke it off?" Mom stormed back into the room. "Are you out of your mind? What is wrong with you? You have a gorgeous woman who is perfect for you and you dump her just before the wedding?"

"I *did* have a woman who was perfect for me, and you drove her away!"

Mom and Dad both gaped at me like I'd gone crazy.

Then the lightbulb came on.

Mom's eyes popped wide and then she let out an aggravated groan. "Oh, good grief! Please do not say this is about Charlie Watson! She broke your heart, Nixon. How can you still be hung up on that girl?"

"She didn't want to break up with me," I retorted.

Mom's face flickered with confusion as I pointed a finger at Dad. "You went and saw her, telling her she was going to ruin my life and destroy the family. You said she wasn't good enough for me. And she believed it! She walked away because she thought she was doing me a favor."

"She was!" Dad's voice reverberated throughout the room. "That girl spelled nothing but disaster for you. She was an airy-fairy dreamer who was leading you astray. I did what was necessary to protect you!"

"What?" Mom touched his arm, clearly oblivious to my father's manipulation. "You never told me this."

"It's what you wanted, Gloria. You were distraught after Nixon told us their travel plans, petrified that we were going to lose him. I had to do something. I couldn't see you suffer that way again." Dad's voice cracked.

My eyebrows dipped together, Dad's wretched expression trying to tug at my sympathy, but I still couldn't move past the fact that he'd interfered. "What did you say to Charlie? Did you threaten her?"

He looked to the floor like he'd just been busted. Mom blinked at me, still trying to process what was going on.

"You scared her off." My voice was low and brittle. "You made up some bullshit story, weaving the perfect lies to drive her away from me!"

Dad smoothed a hand over his hair and patted the back of his head. "It wasn't all lies. Your plans were going to pull the family apart. I told her what you both needed to understand, what *you* weren't willing to hear!"

"What did you say, huh? What threat was the clincher?" My voice was deep with rage.

Dad closed his eyes, then shook his head like I was being a pain in the ass for asking. "I just laid out what your future might look like. You were young and immature, your plans barely thought through. You would have faced so many battles. It would have been too hard, so she left."

"Because you told her to!"

"I didn't tell her she had to go. She made that choice when she said she couldn't look you in the eye and break it off. Come on, son, she was smart enough to know you two were a lost cause. You were the only one who didn't get it."

"Until Shayna." Mom implored me with a look that could have broken the strongest man. But I'd seen it too many times before. I'd given into it...to my own detriment.

Enough was enough.

Pinching the bridge of my nose, I fought for air as a new kind of rage brewed inside me. It was a thunderstorm, and I fed off its power.

Letting out a frustrated yell, I pointed at my parents and went for it. "You convinced me that she was too wild and that's why she left! You made me feel like I wasn't worthy of her!"

"We never!" Mom's voice pitched high. "Honey,

she left without saying goodbye. That was her choice. And I may not have known what your father did, but…" She glanced at Dad. "He said those things to her because he loves us. And she did leave without a word, which hurt you incredibly. She could have handled that so much better."

"Don't you dare!" I pointed at Mom. "Don't you dare judge her when Dad was the one who crossed the line! We could have talked about it! We could have found a compromise, but you drove her away from me and then lied about it!" My voice boomed inside the room, the vein in my forehead no doubt bulging.

Mom blinked, her hand trembling as she covered her mouth.

"We just wanted to protect you." Dad spoke calmly, ever the smooth and cool lawyer. "You're so…important to us, and she had this hold on you. We were scared to lose you. We so want you to have a good life."

"Yeah, a good life," I spat. "One where I'm happy. And you stole that from me. I know you never really liked Charlie. She scared you. You just thought of her as a threat. But you never got it. You never saw how she brought me to life. After Reagan died, she was the first person to make me feel joy again. I was genuinely happy whenever I was with her. How could you take that from me?"

Mom and Dad didn't answer right away, so I kept going.

"You go on and on about wanting me to have a

safe, secure life." I threw my arms up. "I could be whoever I wanted around her and she was going to love me anyway. That was the kind of security I had in her. The only security you've offered me is financial. That's worthless if this is how I'm going to feel for the rest of my life!" I slapped my chest as I spoke. "I am unhappy! I am living a life I don't want, to try and please all you people!"

The raw honesty in my voice shocked them both.

Mom's hand fluttered over her chest as she tried to find her voice.

"How…how can you not be happy?" She trembled. "You have everything you need. We've given you everything!"

"Except love without expectation." I leaned forward, begging her to understand. "Do you have any idea how exhausting it is? I have tried so hard to make you guys proud. To make up for the pain of losing your daughter."

"And you have." Dad went to squeeze my shoulder but I jerked away from him.

"I don't need your pride anymore. I want your acceptance…and your love. But I need to choose my own life, and I need that to be okay with you."

Mom's mouth opened like she wanted to speak, but nothing came out.

Dad's wounded expression made my heart sink.

Closing my eyes, I let out a soft sigh and shook my head. "It's not going to be, is it?"

The only sound in the room was the ticking clock on the mantel. It had never sounded so frickin' loud.

My jaw worked to the side as I shook my head and let out a heavy sigh.

"Well, I'm sorry to disappoint, but it's time for me to do what I should have done years ago. I've strived my whole life to be the perfect son, but I can't carry that responsibility anymore. I want Charlie. I love her. She's the only girl I'm meant to be with. Now I don't give a shit if you want me to or not, but I'm finding that girl and I'm telling her exactly how I feel. And I will frickin' drop to my knees and beg if I have to, until she understands how much I never wanted to let her go."

"What about graduation?" Mom whispered. "You're still going to do that, right? And Columbia? Your future?"

I frowned at her, pissed off yet not surprised that she was of course worrying about fucking law school and not my tattered heart.

Dad's pained expression deepened. "Please, please don't give up this opportunity. You've worked so hard. Get your qualifications and then go wherever the hell you need to. Heck, take Charlie to New York with you if that helps. Please, son. Please don't throw this opportunity away."

I cringed, yet again feeling that pressure and struggling to stand up against it.

I didn't love the idea of law school, but if Charlie came with me…

If Dad was saying they'd accept that…

At the end of the day she was all I wanted. If I could convince her to join me, then I could do it.

And maybe I'd have a chance of keeping both parties happy.

Maybe I could make this work.

With a heavy sigh, I gave them both a stern glare. "If she agrees to come with me, then you will treat her like a queen, you understand me? You will accept the fact that we love each other and you will do *nothing* to break us apart again. Are we agreed?"

Dad's expression was hard, but he relented with a stiff nod.

Mom was still staring at the floor, shock turning her face a stark white.

"Look, I'm sorry about the wedding, Mom. I'm sorry I didn't find the courage to do this earlier. I should never have let it get this far."

"Is Shayna okay?"

"I hope she will be." My chest hurt. I hated that she had become a victim of this fight.

Mom sniffed delicately and tried for a smile. "She's a strong woman. I'm sure she'll be fine."

"I know it's awkward, but divorce would be worse. If you'd just let me follow my heart in the first place, all of this could have been avoided."

She closed her eyes like she was going to throw up and pressed her hand into her stomach.

I wanted to apologize for letting them down, but I just couldn't form the words.

They'd let *me* down.

If anyone had a right to be pissed off, it was me.

Unable to keep looking at their forlorn faces, I made a beeline for my old room. I had no place else to go.

I took the stairs two at a time and shut myself away. I'd hoped to feel liberated by my outburst, but the heavy weight still sat inside me, a painful reminder that this was a bleak day for my family. The joy Mom and Dad had so desperately been waiting for was covered with another gray cloud. It was partly their doing. But it was also mine.

THIRTY-ONE

CHARLIE

For some weird reason, it almost felt like the last day of my life. I couldn't pinpoint why. Maybe because I'd been seeing Troy and Cassie's wedding as my final chapter.

After that, I was off.

Charlie Watson. A new girl. A new life.

I was petrified yet motivated.

Checking my makeup in the mirror, I smoothed my finger under the purple lipstick on my bottom lip and then just sat there gazing at my reflection for a second. I'd bunched my hair into a messy knot to keep it out of my way while I worked, but tendrils of blue hair had fallen free and were framing my face. Fingering one of my curls, I couldn't help a small smile. I really did love my blue-tipped hair.

Nixon had liked it too, I could tell. It was his favorite color. That's why I'd chosen it. Even though I hadn't seen him for years, I'd still tried to keep a part of him with me. Dyeing my hair had been a subtle attempt that only I understood.

I should have probably cut it off before I left, made a clean break.

But I just couldn't do it.

No matter how far I traveled, Nixon would always be there in some way.

Maybe as time passed, my blue hair would come to stand for something else.

The thought was kind of depressing. My shoulders sagged, in sync with my lips.

"Stop it," I whispered. "You can do this. It's time to stop waiting and go. No matter what happens, you go. You go see the world."

My reflection nodded, my purple lips twitching with a smile as a tendril of excitement flittered through me.

"Charlie! Time to get going, sweetie," Dad called from the living room.

I rolled my eyes and grinned. Dad hated tardiness. He wasn't even involved with the wedding, but he wasn't about to let his daughter be late.

Smoothing down my glittery blue skinny pants, I grabbed my gear and headed for the door.

"You all set?"

"Yep." I nodded, smiling when he kissed me on the cheek.

"Love you, my girl."

"Love you too, Dad." I winked and took the keys from his hand. "See you guys *much* later."

"Okay, honey," Mom called from her bedroom window.

I waved at her from the driveway.

"Try to have a little fun while you're there."

"Mom, I'm there to work."

"I know, but have fun anyway." She grinned and blew me a kiss.

I caught it and rubbed it into my cheek before getting into Dad's car.

I'd sold my rust bucket on Craigslist two days before. It was a miracle I got anything for it, but a mechanic with a soft spot for Volkswagens bought it off me. It was a painful sale. Mom spent the whole time wiggling her eyebrows behind his back and mouthing about how hot he was.

Thank God I was leaving the country and she couldn't keep trying to hook me up with random men.

My heart had always belonged to Nixon; I couldn't imagine giving it to anyone else.

In the last few months, I'd come to terms with that and given my heart to a new dream—travel.

It was time for me to go and be Charlie without Nixon.

Chix would officially die on Nixon's wedding day, and I'd be in Hawaii by then, discovering who

I was without him…or even the hope of him.

It was kind of liberating in some ways.

But it still didn't take that icy edge of pain away.

I was hoping that would melt in time.

"Please melt," I whispered as I reversed out of the driveway and drove to my last LA job.

THIRTY-TWO

NIXON

I hadn't seen or spoken to Charlie in three months. Turning up on her doorstep was a ballsy move, but I didn't know what else to do.

Graduation the day before had been freaking painful. Having to explain to my college buddies and their families that I'd dumped my hot fiancée was hard work. My parents' humiliation was impossible to miss. They put on brave smiles, but their silence in the car on the way home had been deafening.

I'd let them down.

I'd let them all down for a girl they didn't even

like.

And I'd never felt so justified.

Clearing my throat, I ran a hand through my hair and walked up the front steps.

"Please still be living here," I whispered, suddenly aware that there was every chance Charlie may have left and moved in with that boyfriend she'd told me about, or moved back to Montana, or skipped the country altogether.

The possibilities were endless.

It sent a lightning bolt right through me and I ended up pounding on the door as soon as I reached it.

"Charlie?" I called when no one answered.

Rubbing my chin, I knocked again, my knuckles stinging in my desperation.

"Excuse me," someone said. "Hey, excuse me!"

I spun around and found a short lady with gray curls and wrinkles around her eyes peering out her front door.

"Can I help you?" She frowned.

"Oh." I pointed my thumb over my shoulder. "I was just looking for Charlie."

The lady's forehead wrinkled.

"Charlotte Watson. I thought she lived here."

"Sorry, but she moved out about a week ago."

"Oh." I nodded, looking down to hide my searing disappointment. "Do you…do you know where I might be able to find her?"

"I'm pretty sure she's at her wedding today."

"Her wedding?" The words were like a broadsword slashing straight through me.

"Yeah, I heard them talking as they carried their stuff away. All wedding chatter. Excited for the big day. You should have seen the diamond on her finger. It's beautiful."

I couldn't breathe.

It couldn't be happening.

"Are you alright?" The screen door creaked as the lady opened it a little wider and stepped out to check on me.

"Yeah, I'm fine," I clipped, shooting down the stairs before she could reach me. "Thank you for your help."

I tried to run to my car, but my legs felt like slugs. My hand shook as I unlocked the door and slipped into the driver's seat.

"Shit." I whispered, gripping the wheel and unleashing a shout. "SHIT!"

I banged the wheel until I was a puffing mess, then rested my forehead against it.

I was too late.

The love of my life was going off to marry some guy who had given her diamonds.

"She's not even a diamond girl!" I yelled, hating that he didn't know her well enough.

A diamond on Charlie was laughable. I couldn't even picture it. If I ever had the chance to marry her, I'd slip a moonstone or an opal ring on her finger, something untraditional and perfect for her.

Why'd she say yes?

Was it a reaction to my engagement?

Did she do it because she thought I didn't want her anymore?

"You can't do this, Charlie. I want you. I want you!"

Snatching my phone, I started hunting for her number. After ten minutes, I finally found it on the *All About the Bride and Groom* website. I dialed the number and tapped my finger on the wheel…while it went straight to her voice mail message.

"Dammit!"

I gripped my phone and went to throw it on the seat when another idea hit me.

Pulling back up the website, I called Sarah, the girl who'd been working with us to plan Shayna's big day. I dreaded speaking to her, but hopefully she'd have a good idea where I could find Charlie. Hell, if Charlie was getting married, she would have planned the damn thing.

"Hello?"

"Hi, Sarah. It's Nixon. Nixon Holloway?"

"Hello?" She spoke a little louder.

"Sarah? Can you hear me? I'm looking for Charlie."

"Charlie? She's on her way to St. Patrick's for the wedding. I'm sorry, I didn't catch who this was."

"St. Patrick's in town?"

"Hello?"

I gritted my teeth, fighting the urge to scream into the phone.

"Hello? Sorry, I can't really hear you." She let out a disgusted huff. "Justin, my phone's acting up again."

There was a scuffle of noise, and then Justin was

in my ear. "H-hello? Can you hear me?"

"Yes, can you hear me?" I shouted. "Is Charlie getting married?"

"Hello? It must be bad reception," Justin mumbled. "My phone was acting up before too."

"Shit," I muttered, giving up and dropping the phone onto the passenger seat. I leaned my head back.

St. Patrick's. If it was the place I was thinking of, it was a big-ass cathedral-like church.

"*So* not Charlie," I muttered.

How could she do it?

I couldn't let her do it.

I loved her too much to let her fall into the same trap as me. Even if she didn't want me, I still had to stop the wedding. Or at least I had to see her face and know for sure that she wanted to marry this guy.

Lurching forward, I fired up the engine and nearly laughed when "Crashed the Wedding" blasted through my speakers.

There was that music again, telling me what to do.

Turning up the volume, I revved the engine and powered my way into town.

The map on my phone led me to St. Patrick's easily. I parked up on the curb, not even bothering to lock the car as I sprinted up the wide concrete steps and busted into the church.

As soon as I reached the aisle and saw her standing there in a lavish white gown next to some tall guy in a penguin suit, I yelled, "Stop! Everyone stop!"

THIRTY-THREE

CHARLIE

My heart jumped into my throat as everyone in the magnificent church gasped and turned around to see who the crazy person was running down the aisle.

Leaning around the pillar I'd been resting against to take some wide shots of the couple beneath the stunning stained-glass windows, I gaped and nearly choked on my own surprise.

"Nixon?" I whispered.

"You can't do this. You can't marry this guy." His voice trembled with conviction as he reached Cassie and gently spun her around to face him. If I hadn't been so dumbstruck, I would have cracked up laughing.

"Hey!" Troy pushed his shoulder while Cole stepped up from his best man post, ready to grab Nixon and wrestle him out of the building.

Nixon blinked and looked at the two towering guys before glancing down at the bride.

He froze for a second, and then his eyes bulged bigger than I'd ever seen them. "Oh, shi…."

He let Cassie go like she was on fire and stumbled back, nearly falling on his ass. "You're not her." He winced, then looked to Troy. "Okay, um, man, I am *so* sorry. I thought… This is the wrong wedding." He swallowed and looked about ready to puke with embarrassment.

A snort came from the front row followed by a soft slap. Nessa…or Ronnie. They were no doubt fighting giggles. The sound set Jimmy off. He was standing behind Troy and didn't hold back. His loud laughter boomed through the church.

Troy turned and gave his brother a dry glare, but it quickly turned into a snickering grin when Felix joined the pack of hyenas.

It didn't take long for laughter to ripple through the entire church.

Poor Nixon.

He looked like he wanted the ground to open up and swallow him.

And it only got worse when Cassie started shaking her head and backing away from Troy. "This is just another sign," she whimpered.

"Hey, no." Troy jumped after her, grabbing her

hand and putting a quick stop to the retreat.

Gently cupping her cheek, he forced her to look at him. I couldn't see his face, but he was probably smiling with a tenderness that only Troy possessed.

"I know we've had some roadblocks, but this is it. This is *our* day. And I'm not letting some psycho set on reenacting *The Graduate* stop me from marrying the woman I love."

A hush settled across the crowd as all eyes landed on the couple.

Lifting the camera, I quietly snapped a few pictures—capturing the beauty that Troy was creating with his heartfelt speech.

"I love you, Cassie. I always will. And I want you and me…and Felix." He glanced over his shoulder, making Felix blush with a shy smile. "I want us to be an official family. I want it on paper, signed and sealed that you are Mrs. Cassie Baker."

Cassie's lips twitched, her voice trembling when she finally found it. "But it's been so hard getting here."

"I know, but we're here now. We never gave up, because we're meant to be together. And I'm gonna keep fighting for that reality no matter what comes our way." He leaned forward and kissed her while a soft murmur of approval rippled through the crowd.

My lens ended up on Nixon and my breath caught. He had tears in his eyes.

"I'm so sorry," he whispered again, squeezing the back of his neck and giving the couple a pained smile. "Please, get married."

Cassie turned, her frown a mixture of confusion and pity.

But then she smiled at him. "I will."

He cringed and apologized yet again before spinning and practically running for the exit.

He was about halfway down when he spotted Kelly and jerked to a stop.

Her smile was sweet and sympathetic as she pointed to the pillar I was standing behind.

I stepped out of hiding and raised my hand at him.

The look on his face nearly made me cry.

But I was working, and I wasn't going to let those eyes own me again.

I nearly turned away from him and got back to taking photos, but I just couldn't do it. With a flick of my head, I ushered him across to me.

He scampered down the aisle while everyone's eyes tracked him.

As Nixon hid behind the pillar, the gazes all landed on me.

"Sorry about that." I gave them my best smile. "I'll explain later, but why don't we let these two lovebirds finally get married. Third time lucky, right?" A cheer went up from the crowd and I raised my camera to snap photos of their hilarious expressions. Hopefully Cassie and Troy would look back on the moment with a smile and a laugh.

Leaning into a row of seats, I zoomed in on the bride and groom and caught Troy's sweet, reassuring smile, then managed to get the look on Cassie's face.

The service resumed and I snapped some more pictures, then glanced at Nixon. He leaned in and softly whispered, "I'm sorry. I thought you were getting married."

I threw him an incredulous look.

"Your next-door neighbor said… And then Sarah…"

"What's Sarah got to do with it?"

Oh man, I wondered where she was. She'd be ready to throttle Nixon for nearly throwing off the *third* wedding attempt.

"Ugh." Nixon softly groaned. "It's… It was…a miscommunication."

"How could you think I was getting married?" I whispered before turning away to snap a shot of the wedding party as they all bowed their heads to pray.

"You said you had a boyfriend." His whisper was so soft I barely heard it. And then it took me a moment to remember I'd told him that, which meant he figured out my lie within a nanosecond. His deep frown was kind of cute and I quickly snapped a photo of it.

He placed his hand on mine and gently pushed the camera down and away from my face. "I have to talk to you. I can't keep pretending like there isn't something between us. It's driving me insane."

I stilled, then caught sight of Sarah out of the corner of my eye. She was eyeing me from the other side of the church, an irritated frown on her face. I quickly lifted the camera and snapped a few more photos. Thank God the camera was covering my face as I tried to process what the hell Nixon was saying to me.

Three months of nothing and he just turns up like this?

The minister said "Amen" and the crowd all cast their eyes back to the couple while they got ready to exchange their vows. I had to move into a better position.

Glancing at Nixon, I grimaced and whisper-barked, "What about Shayna?"

"We broke up." He brushed his fingers over the back of my hand. "I've been trying to figure everything out…but I know now. I know what I want."

Damn those brown eyes. They were going to make me fold before I could stop myself.

Looking away from them, I noticed Troy had already started speaking. "Look, in case you haven't noticed, I'm working right now. This is a really bad time."

"I'll wait."

I walked away from his soft promise and moved into a better position. Once Cassie was done, they'd exchange rings and then kiss. I couldn't miss a second of that. Even though the posed photos were coming later, I still had to capture *the* wedding kiss.

Nixon hung back in the shadows while I moved into the center aisle and tried to be invisible.

Cassie and Troy only had eyes for each other. Her voice trembled with emotion as she said her vows. His smile was like the sun, his eyes gleaming as he gazed down at her.

When the minister finally said, "You may now kiss the bride," I planted my finger and snapped as much of the kiss as I could. I'd changed it to a high speed setting and was confident at least one shot would be pure gold.

The lighting in the place was freaking ethereal. I couldn't wait to go through the photos and touch them all up before I left for Hawaii.

I'd be pulling an all-nighter to do it, but I could sleep on the plane, right?

I glanced to the side of the church and spotted Nixon watching me. His smile was sad yet hopeful, which only served to act as a sledgehammer to my gut.

What the hell did he want to say to me?

I thought I'd never see him again, and there he was, busting down a church door to stop me from marrying someone.

It was ridiculously romantic, and totally confusing.

He'd broken up with Shayna. When?

Did I even want to hear the story?

I was set on leaving the country. Finally letting go of the hold he had on me.

Slamming my teeth together, I got back to work, hoping that staying busy and ignoring him would be enough to get me through the rest of the wedding.

Although, I had a sinking suspicion Nixon wasn't going anywhere in a hurry.

I saw the look on his face when he said he

needed to talk.

I just hoped I was strong enough to handle whatever the hell it was he wanted to say to me.

THIRTY-FOUR

NIXON

The wedding was slow and painful. Charlie basically ignored me while she worked.

Fair enough. She was getting paid to do a job and I wasn't going to get in the way of that.

But I wasn't leaving either.

I'd shadow her until I had a chance to say what I needed to.

The bride and groom were nice enough to let me hover, despite the wedding planner's complaints. After a little sweet-talking from Charlie, Sarah capitulated, but I was pretty sure she wouldn't talk to, or smile at, me for the rest of the event. Not only was I the guy who nearly ruined a perfectly planned wedding, but I was also the guy who'd pulled out last minute of another wedding they'd been planning.

Scum was too nice of a word to describe me.

I went and apologized to Justin and he was pretty good about it. Thankfully the groom had redeemed the day with his beautiful speech, so the wedding was saved, and I was only responsible for destroying Shayna's big day.

I cringed and gripped the back of my neck, unsure I'd ever live down my shame and guilt.

"Just focus on Charlie, man," I mumbled. "You did the right thing."

After the wedding, the bridal party drove straight to the reception venue. I followed Mr. Watson's car, making sure never to lose sight of Charlie. The afternoon was whiled away on the vast grounds of Hasley Gardens, an exclusive private property that was hired out for weddings and special functions. It was down a mile-long driveway, and you wouldn't even know it existed unless someone told you about it. They must have waited months for this booking.

Shit, I can't believe I nearly fucked it up for them.

Thankfully, the bride had relaxed more and more as the afternoon wore on. The groom and his son (at least I assumed he was his son) knew how to make her laugh, and the three of them were obviously a close-knit family. She looked stunning in her designer dress, surrounded by meticulous greenery and water features. Troy couldn't take his eyes off her…or lose the dopey smile on his face.

I got it. I felt the same way as I watched Charlie take charge and work her magic with the camera. She didn't pose them too much; most of the time she just pointed at a pretty area in the gardens and told them to go have a chat. Occasionally she'd call out for them to kiss, cuddle or touch foreheads, but most of the time she got trigger-happy catching moments of spontaneous beauty. The bridal party was small, but their respective partners had been invited to join in the fun.

The flower girl was pretty darn cute too with her blonde ringlets and blue eyes…plus those dimples. She had enough charm and character to mingle with the wedding party easily. Her dad hovered around, reeling her in with a quiet Aussie accent. "Angel, come here, gorgeous."

She'd run to him with a giggle and he'd hoist her into the air.

Charlie snapped a bunch of those photos. I caught a glimpse of one of them over her shoulder and it was photographic genius.

That light. Charlie would be going nuts over that light.

A breathy giggle spurted out of her before she lifted her camera again.

I stood back with a proud smile and kept watching it all from the sidelines.

Glasses of champagne, easy banter, and raucous laughter mixed with piles of love. It made for an entertaining afternoon.

The photos would be amazing, I had no doubt

about that.

Where I could, I lent a hand, but most of the wedding party acted like I didn't exist…or threw me the odd *you're a weirdo* look. The only reason they were letting me hang around was because Charlie asked them too.

As the night approached and the wedding reception got underway, I stuck to the shadows and the corners of the room as much as I could.

Kelly bought me a beer during the dinner service, her eyes dancing with amusement.

"I didn't think you were capable of something that crazy."

"We've met like one time before this." I shrugged, hinting that she didn't know me at all.

"Yet I've spent hours hearing all about you."

My lips twitched.

Kelly grinned and sipped her wine. "Finally figured out you love her, huh?"

"I've always known," I murmured. "It's just taken me a while to find the courage to fight for it."

Kelly's expression softened. "Well, good luck. And make sure you say everything you need to, tonight."

"Why?"

She went to answer me but was stopped by a girl I didn't recognize. She was blonde with these stunning blue eyes that checked me out before speaking. "What's the deal? Are you really here to win Charlie over? Because if you're not sure, you can just walk your butt right out the door."

I frowned at the strange woman and flicked a

glance at Kelly.

She grinned and introduced us. "Nixon, this is Fliss, Charlie's roommate."

Fliss stuck out her hand to shake and I caught a glimpse of that big ring the neighbor had mentioned.

"Nice ring." I shook her hand with a small grin.

"Thank you." She spun it on her finger and nailed me with a stellar glare. "Now, stop changing the subject and tell me what your intentions are."

"I…" I let out a sigh. "My intentions are to tell her that I love her."

Fliss planted her fist on her hip. "Aren't you supposed to be getting married at the end of June?"

"I called off the wedding."

Her eyebrows rose, her eyes still fiery with concern. "Did you tell your parents?"

Shit, Charlie really hadn't held back, had she?

I looked to the floor with a heavy sigh. "I didn't know what my dad had done to her. I just found out and, uh… They know I'm not happy about it. They know I have no intention of getting back together with Shayna."

Fliss nodded, slightly appeased, but not enough to smile at me. "Well, that's something, but don't come into this half-assed. It's not fair when she's—"

Fliss's warning was cut off by Jimmy Baker, the lead guitarist for Chaos, calling everyone to gather around for the bride and groom's first dance. Kelly grinned and quickly grabbed Fliss's arm, pulling her away from me. She whispered something into

Kelly's ear, and Charlie's cousin nodded before they both glanced over their shoulders at me.

More eye bulging and head shakes. I was seeing a lot of that.

Slumping down into a spare chair against the wall, I got out of the way while the bride and groom did their wedding dance to "Say You Won't Let Go." The song hit me right in the heart, like it did everyone. Jimmy was singing in perfect harmony with Ness while the rest of the band quietly played behind them. Troy's son was also up there, which was a nice touch.

I studied their faces, saw them smiling into the crowd while they played. Seemed like everyone had a partner. The bride and groom swayed next to each other, and as the song continued, different couples walked onto the floor. The tall guy who looked like Superman with his little wife. They'd been at the photo shoot. I was pretty sure her name was Ella.

Next to her was a blonde woman with her… Shit, that was Sean Jaxon, the Hollywood film star.

My eyebrows popped high as I soaked in the fame for a second.

"You're funny." A little voice over my shoulder made me jump.

I turned and spotted a girl with blonde ringlets and a cherub face.

"Hi, flower girl."

"Hello." She brushed a curl off her cheek and stuck out her hand. "I'm Angel. What's your name, funny man?"

"Nixon."

She bobbed her head and climbed onto the chair next to me, tucking her silky dress beneath her knees. Her feet dangled above the ground, her sparkly shoes swinging back and forth.

"I'm six." Her cute little nose twitched.

"Wow. That's pretty old."

"I know. I go to school now."

"You must be pretty smart, then."

"Daddy says so." She pointed to the dance floor at a good-looking guy with a super-hot wife. He was the Australian guy at the photo shoot.

Leo? Yeah, that was it.

His wife was blonde and brilliant. Her smile could light a room.

"You know, you look like your mommy."

Angel grinned like I'd just given her the world's best compliment. "Thank you."

I gazed back at the couple. They had their foreheads pressed together as they swayed to the song, his hand gently caressing her baby bump.

"My little brother's in her belly. He's coming out in two months."

"You must be excited."

She shrugged. "I already have a little sister, Elenore. She's two and can be really annoying, but she's cute so that makes it easier to love her."

I grinned. "Elenore. Nice name."

"Yeah, they named her after that song by The Turtles. My parents do that." She shrugged. "I'm named after that song 'Angelia' by Richard Marx. Who knows what they'll call my brother." She shook her head like her parents were a hopeless case.

I couldn't help laughing.

She looked at me with a *what's so funny* expression and I quickly covered. "So, having a little sister is sometimes fun and sometimes not."

"Yep." She nodded. "Mostly fun, I guess. Except when she gets together with Aunt Ella and Uncle Cole's kids." Her eyes bulged. "They're like the terrible trio."

Angel was adorable, and it was hard not to chuckle at her serious sweetness. "And how old are Aunt Ella and Uncle Cole's kids?"

"They're three. Twin boys. You can only imagine." She rolled her eyes.

"Lucky you get to go to school and get away from them, huh?"

"For sure." She nodded, then beamed and waved at the blonde lady dancing with Sean Jaxon.

The woman gave me a cautious glare. I reciprocated with a closed-mouth smile, which she accepted, but I had a feeling once the song was done, she'd be coming to collect the little cutie beside me.

"That's Aunt Morgan. She's teaching me how to dance."

"Nice." I nodded. "You like dancing? Why aren't you up there with your family, then?"

"I'll go soon. I just thought you looked a little lonely." She scratched the side of her nose. "My best friend, Thomas, he looks like that sometimes. That's how I became his friend."

"Oh yeah?"

"Yeah, he was sitting by himself one day so I went to say hello because Mommy says that we should always make people try to smile, and he wasn't smiling." She brushed at the curl that kept tickling her cheek before continuing with her story. "He's my best friend now because he's smart and we like the same stuff."

"Well, that's always a good start. Best friends like the same things."

"Yeah, I know." She grinned. "I wish he was here. It'd be nice to have someone my size to dance with."

I glanced up at the floor and noticed Angel's dad frowning at me. Fair enough. I was the crazy guy who had tried to stop the wedding.

Pointing at him, I leaned down and spoke to Angel. "I can see a guy over there who'd probably dance with you."

She giggled and hopped down from the chair. "You know, Mom thinks what you did was romantic, but Daddy says you're bloody crazy."

I laughed, then winced. "Maybe a little of both?"

She grinned and waved at me. "Goodbye, crazy man."

"Thanks for making me smile, Angel."

She stopped at my words, her face like the star on top of a Christmas tree. Running back, she went on her tiptoes and kissed my cheek before racing into her father's arms.

He crouched down to collect her and she wrapped her arms and legs around him while they danced on the floor together.

It was a thing of beauty…and Charlie captured it all.

Standing up, she gazed at her camera display with a triumphant smile before continuing to snap more precious moments.

I had no idea how many hundreds of photos she must have taken throughout the day, but she was going all out for this wedding.

I wanted to see them, to pour over them like we used to. The hours we'd spend at her computer manipulating images while music blasted out of her stereo. Her mom would bustle in to turn it down, but as new songs started we'd slowly increase the volume again.

I missed those days. The Snickers bars, the movie-a-thons, the photos, the music.

We could never get those moments back. But I hoped like hell we could make new ones.

My chest constricted as Chaos started a rock version of "Happy Together." Charlie and I loved this version. We'd sing it all the time at high school and I'd imagine myself with her forever.

She glanced across the room and caught my eye. Once again we were transported to that place where we belonged.

My lips rose with a smile but her sad expression, and the way her gaze hit the floor, threw a noose around my hope. I'd imagined it differently. Thought the fact that I'd busted in on a wedding was enough to prove how much I wanted her.

But something was holding her back.

And I was almost too afraid to find out what it was.

THIRTY-FIVE

CHARLIE

Cheers went up as Cassie and Troy drove away for the first night of their honeymoon. Felix was staying with Chaos while they were away, which, according to Kelly, made Cassie kind of nervous. But Fliss promised she'd make sure everyone behaved themselves.

I rolled my eyes and grinned. Poor Felix was going to get lumped with like seven temporary parents. Just what every teenager wants.

"You okay?" Kelly's long arm settled around my shoulders.

I bobbed my head, but a nervous swallow gave

me away. "He's still here, isn't he?"

"Yep." She accentuated the P. "He's helping Chaos with the pack-up."

"And they don't mind?"

"He's the guy who busted in on a wedding. They think he's awesome."

I snickered and shook my head. "I can't believe he did that. I thought he was getting married. I've been trying to let him go. I'm moving on." My voice pitched high as I rushed to a finish.

"I know." She squeezed me against her and kissed my forehead. She was ridiculously tall in those heels. "Remember, just because he's here proclaiming his love for you doesn't mean you have to change all of your plans for him." Spinning me to face her, she looked me in the eye. "This is your life. And I know you'll always love him, but don't give up on this travel dream just because he's here. See something through, Charlie. I beg you. If your love is real, he'll be waiting for you when you get back."

I bit my lip, then wrinkled my nose. "You're not just saying that to get me home early, are you?"

With a soft snort, she pulled me into a tight hug. "I just want you to be happy."

"Thanks, Kels." I squeezed her back, suddenly missing her before I'd even left.

Letting me go, she kissed my cheek and then propelled me towards the fairy-lit reception hall where things were slowly being packed away.

I ambled back into the room and spotted Nixon chatting with Ralphie. The bass player said something that made Nixon smile, and then Flick added his own quip that had all three of them chuckling. They all looked to Jace, who was oblivious to whatever they were talking about. He was transfixed by an African-American waitress who was carrying a tray of dirty champagne glasses. She glanced his way, her lips twitching with a grin, before disappearing through the service doors.

Jace looked down, his full lips fighting a smile.

Flick said something and Jace's cheeks bloomed hot red, making all the guys crack up laughing again.

Except Nixon.

Because he'd noticed me on the other side of the room.

Our eyes locked and I suddenly couldn't breathe.

This was it. The moment I'd been waiting for.

And it was the world's worst timing.

"Hey," Nixon said when he finally reached me.

Over his shoulder, I caught a few curious gazes, so I tipped my head towards the door. We stepped outside and took the path on the right, walking along it until we were completely alone. The reception hall was surrounded by copious gardens. During the day, people paid to walk the different pathways and admire the carefully maintained flowers and sculpted hedges, but late at night it was an empty, moonlit oasis. The warm summer air caressed my skin while crickets and other insects created a soundtrack for our silent walk. I knew I had to speak at some point, but I wasn't ready until we found a private little nook within a waist-high maze of hedges. Moonlight bathed the patch of grass in the middle and I took a seat, crossing my legs and studying Nixon as he eased to the ground beside me. He propped his elbows onto his knees and looked at me.

I loved the way the moonlight played off his features, casting shadows, highlighting the angular structure of his face. I was tempted to take a photo, but sometimes even the best photographer can't capture the beauty of the moment. I pulled my camera off and laid it on the ground beside me.

"You really knocked it out of the park with the whole *Graduate* routine."

Nixon snickered and shook his head. "'Crashed the Wedding' was playing in the car as I raced to find you. I guess it kind of inspired me."

I grinned. "I love that song."

"Me too." His voice was serious as he turned to face me and gently took my hands. "Just more proof."

"Of what?"

"That we're meant to be together."

"Because we like the same song?"

"You know it's not just that." He pressed his lips together, then gave me a pained look. "Why didn't you tell me what Dad said to you? Why didn't you come find me? We could have worked it out together."

I pulled my hands from his and tucked them under my legs. "So you found out, then."

"Yeah, I found out."

"Is that why you dumped her?"

"No." He shook his head. "I discovered the truth *as* I was dumping her." His sigh was heavy. He propped his elbows back onto his knees. "I just couldn't keep pretending anymore. I've been miserable since the day you left. I tried to find my happy within that, but then you came back into the picture and just reminded me how much better my life was with *you*."

His words made my eyes tingle and sheen. I blinked and looked up at the moon. "Maybe I never should have left, but…they were going to make it really hard. Your dad threatened to put a restraining order against me and get people to write horrible things about me in the media. He described the flow-on effect really well. And he also said he was going to cut you off financially."

Nixon's eyes rounded before he dipped his head and softly cursed.

Okay, so he hadn't found out *everything*, then.

I winced, hoping I hadn't made it worse. "You know, I don't know whether he would have gone through with it or not, but it was enough to make me realize that it'd be a battle over you. And I just couldn't put any of us in that position. My parents have had to deal with family shit their whole lives, and it sucks. I didn't want that for you. After everything your family already lost…" I sighed and started picking at the grass. "I never realized I'd be taking your heart with me though."

He turned to face me, his shadowed expression

wrinkled with pain.

"How could you not know that?" His deep voice sent a shiver down my spine. He said the words with such strength and conviction. It made me feel like a fool for believing his father so easily.

But then it also made me warm on the inside.

He loved me.

He'd never stopped.

"Charlie." His voice was husky as he brushed his knuckles across my knee. "Did you honestly not know how much you meant to me?"

I shrugged. "You were always so much better than I was. I never felt worthy of you in the first place. I just figured you'd get over me and find someone else." I glanced up and swallowed. "And you did. You found Shayna."

"But she's not you." He cupped my cheeks and gently turned me to face him. "It's only ever been you. You're my best friend. The love of my life."

His lips were soft and inviting as they touched mine.

I sank into the kiss, gripping his wrists when he deepened it. I closed my eyes and the world disappeared. All that existed was Nixon.

It would have been so easy to stay trapped in that bubble, floating over life like none of it mattered.

But we couldn't do that.

Tents had doors.

Vacations had endings.

And life was full of shitty situations that couldn't be dreamed away.

As if to prove my point, Nixon pulled back and whispered words that I couldn't agree to. "Come to New York with me. Make me the happiest man alive."

Tears welled in my eyes as I leaned my forehead against his. "I can't, Nix. I'm leaving."

"What?" The sadness in his voice made my heart squeeze.

"I'm all booked. I'm flying out tomorrow." I sniffed, keeping my head dipped so he couldn't see the onset of tears.

"Where are you going?"

"Hawaii, and then on to…I'm not sure yet. I've got a pretty long list and I'll book as I go."

With his knuckle, he nudged my chin up so he could see my face. His smile was sad yet beautiful. "Finally chasing those dreams, huh?"

"Trying to," I whispered. "I can't pull out last minute."

"I know. I wouldn't want you to." His voice was soft and deep. Soft and sexy.

My insides stirred with desire. I could have seriously drowned in those moonlit eyes. They were dark pools of love and longing.

His thumb was feather light on the tip of my chin. "How long will you be gone?"

"I don't know." My breath hitched as the tears trickled free.

Nixon clenched his jaw and looked out into the darkness.

Slashing the tears off my cheeks, I wanted to lighten the moment with a lame joke. But I couldn't think of a single thing to make him smile.

Reaching for his face, I traced his cheekbones—so familiar yet new.

And then I whispered something I didn't even see coming.

"But we've got tonight."

My heart must have wanted to say it, because as the words slipped out, they suddenly felt like the most important ones I'd ever said.

Nixon and I were obviously destined not to be together for long. But we'd make the most of the moments we were given.

His brown eyes caught my expression and he smiled at me, one of those tender smiles that always melted my heart. Gently taking my arms, he dragged me off the grass and onto his lap. I straddled him, awed by my overwhelming love for this guy.

Brushing his lips with my thumb, I murmured, "I love you."

He responded by cupping the back of my head and pulling me into a kiss. And it wasn't just any kiss. It was the kind of kiss I could soak in, like a hot bath at the end of a stressful day.

It was the kind of kiss that would see me through months of separation.

It was the kiss that said *I'm yours*.

Our lips trembled against each other, heat quickly building as we lost ourselves in the moonlight. Nixon set my hair free of the messy bun and curled his fingers into my wild locks. His other hand trailed from my shoulder and down to my breast.

He gave it a gentle squeeze and laughed into my mouth.

I pulled back with a curious grin and he squeezed me again.

"Still the perfect size," he murmured.

I laughed with him, loving him more than anyone ever could. "Still all yours."

With a wink, I pulled my shirt off, exposing my bright blue bra.

"It matches your hair." He grinned, then kissed me between my collarbones. His lips were warm and delicious. As soon as his tongue hit my soft skin and trailed a line down between my breasts, my entire body started buzzing.

He unhooked my bra and the warm breeze tickled my sensitive spots, adding to my euphoria when his tongue curled around my nipple. I tipped my neck back with an unchecked moan.

Nixon's strong hands supported my back while I gripped his shoulders and melted into a puddle of desire. Heat pooled between my legs as an urgency to have him tore through me.

But I couldn't do that.

Because this was our last time in a while and I wanted to take it slow, draw it out, enjoy every second of it.

Opening my eyes, I smiled up at the moon before threading my fingers into Nixon's hair and tipping his head up. I wanted his mouth on mine again.

He obliged, his warm tongue both a comfort and

a turn-on.

I wanted to memorize the feeling.

Because I wanted to make this moment last forever.

THIRTY-SIX

NIXON

Charlie's tongue in my mouth felt so damn right. I never wanted to stop touching her, kissing her. But the reality was, I'd have to.

I shoved the thought from my mind, not wanting to ruin the moment or get too far ahead of myself. All that mattered was her, me…us.

I sank into the kiss, pulling her against me and relishing the feel of her beautiful breasts pressing into my chest. I needed them on my skin, so I quickly pulled out of the kiss and yanked off my shirt. Charlie helped me, throwing the fabric aside before gluing our bodies back together. We groaned in unison, the touch of flesh on flesh stirring old flames that were growing hotter by the second.

A strong part of me wanted to devour her, to tear the clothes off her body and have her hot and fast. But I also wanted to savor the moment, draw it out and make it last as long as I could.

It was our last time for who knew how long. It had to be the best time we'd ever had.

Supporting her back, I flipped her over onto the grass. Her hair splayed out in the moonlight. Paired with the glowing of her skin, she looked like a painting I'd hang on my wall.

"You are so beautiful," I whispered.

She gave me her classic smile, which only enriched her beauty.

I loved her so much. I'd never stop.

Trailing kisses down her neck, I sucked her nipples the way she liked it, then slowly stripped the rest of her clothes off her body. Each time a new bit of flesh was exposed, I kissed it, tasted it, memorized the shape. She soon lay naked beneath me and I took my time pleasuring her, caressing, kissing, nibbling every inch of her until she was arching her back beneath me. Her moans of pleasure filled the private garden, sinking into the hedges around us and filling the air like a sweet song.

Gripping my hair, she dragged me up her body. "I need you…now."

Snatching my jeans, I scrambled for protection.

She giggled. "You figured you'd get lucky

tonight, huh?"

"I was knocking on your door to tell you I love you always and forever. A guy comes prepared for that kind of thing."

Her laugh deepened to that adorable chuckle I couldn't get enough of. I went still, soaking it in before she yanked the condom out of my grasp and helped me wrap myself.

Then she lay back down and gave me every last inch of her.

Sliding home was the best feeling I'd had in years. It was familiar yet driven by a new intensity that was powerful and sweet.

"Damn, you feel good," I whispered against her ear before sucking her lobe and sinking even further into her.

"Welcome home," she whispered, digging her fingers into my back and urging me to drive harder.

Her panting breath on my cheek was soft yet electric. She trailed her lips across my jawline and sucked my chin as I rose and thrust back and forth.

Delicate fingers rested against my forearms as she gazed at me with a dreamy smile. She opened her mouth to speak, but all she could manage was a deep moan that soon gave way to a whimpering cry of pleasure. Grabbing my ass, she pushed me inside her until I was driving hard and fast to a place I'd never been before.

Sex had sent me to high places, but this one was a whole new level.

Her cries grew and I joined her, forgetting the

fact that we were exposed to the night.

All that existed was me and her.

My eyes glazed as an orgasm rocketed through me. I pushed into her and held fast as she gripped my body, wrapping her legs around me and holding tight.

As I slowly floated back to reality, my arms went slack and I lay on top of her, tantalized by the brush of her erect nipples on my skin. She cupped the back of my head and nestled our cheeks together, using my body as a naked blanket for hers.

Her lips quivered against my earlobe, and then I felt a tear trickle between our cheeks.

I tried to pull away so I could look at her, but she held tight and kept me where I was.

"I'm okay," she whispered. "I was just thinking that if we have to have a goodbye, this is the perfect one." She sniffed. "When I leave you tonight, I won't be tormented like the other times. We love each other. I know that now. And we're not being torn apart by outside forces."

I wrestled against her and pulled back so I could stare into her eyes.

Running my finger down the edge of her face, I braved a smile. "I'll wait for you. I don't care how long you need to be away."

Her smile was wonky. "I can't ask you to wait."

"You're not. I'm choosing to."

"But…"

"I know that you're the only girl for me now, and *nothing* is going to persuade me otherwise."

She cupped my cheek and brushed her thumb beneath my eye. "You're the only guy for me too. There's never been anyone but you."

Her eyes told me exactly what she was saying. And I was honored.

My throat thickened with emotion as I gave her the best smile I could.

But it was hampered by the growing sadness.

She was leaving me again. Yes, she'd come back, but when? How much longer did I have to live without her?

"You'll stay in touch, right?" I croaked, panic stealing my voice.

She let out a breathy chuckle and nodded. "I'll send you songs, photos. I'll GoPro everything."

I laughed and rested my forehead against hers. "I'll write you love letters."

My husky words scored me a kiss. It was deep and passionate, an outpouring of emotion that took us on another ride. One last moment of beauty before we pulled our clothes back on and went our separate ways.

We exchanged numbers, something that made us both chuckle. How had we spent so much time together, gotten to the point where we'd declared our love for each other, without doing something so simple, so mundane, as exchanging numbers? She made me promise not to see her off at the airport. I understood why and so I agreed, as long as she promised to text me as soon as she landed in Hawaii.

We kissed again by her car, and it took

everything in me not to beg her to stay.

As her car disappeared into the darkness, I felt my gut sink into my shoes. The sadness that enveloped me was a new kind. It wasn't a confused or desolate sadness. There was a thread of hope that kept me from sinking.

Charlie was still mine.

And I was hers.

And one day, we'd be together again.

THIRTY-SEVEN

CHARLIE

"You sure you don't want to change your mind?"

"Fliss, don't." I gave her a stern look, wishing I hadn't asked her and Flick to drive me to the airport.

My mom, although she wanted me to go, was a wreck. It was finally hitting home that her flighty daughter was seriously seeing something through and she may not be back anytime soon. Dad suggested we say goodbye at home so that I'd have time to mop up my tears in the car.

It was an effort. Mom's tears set me off, and then

having to hug Papa Bear goodbye sucked. He was really sweet and stoic about it, but as the car pulled away, I noticed him blinking really fast.

Fliss and Flick were quiet at first, but as we entered LAX, she started talking and wouldn't shut up.

"I can't go back now." My voice shook. "Everything's in place. This is right. I have to go."

She nodded, looking kind of sad. "At least you have something to come back for now."

I let out a watery laugh, clamping my lips together to shut off the sound. I couldn't think about Nixon or I'd lose it completely.

I hadn't slept a wink the night before. I didn't even get home until after three, and then I distracted myself by working through Cassie and Troy's photos. I didn't finish but had my laptop fully charged for the plane.

The early afternoon was fast approaching and I still hadn't caught a wink. I'd probably crash on the plane. Man, I hoped so. Zero sleep always made me tearful. I didn't want to show up in Hawaii a blubbering mess.

Flick pulled the car into an unloading bay and I slid out, my legs acting like iron beams—slow and unbendable.

"Here you go, travel girl." Flick handed me my pack and I tried not to crumple under its weight.

Pulling it on, I hitched it onto my shoulders and nodded, double-checking I had everything.

Fliss reached for my hand. "You want me to come in with you? Flick can park the car…"

I was shaking my head before she could finish. "Don't, please. I just need to get this underway on my own."

She gave me a reluctant nod, crossing her arms and obviously holding back a tirade of *I don't want you going on your own. It's not safe. Nixon loves you. Stay. Stay. Stay!*

"Thanks for everything, you guys." I gave them a sad smile and stepped into Flick's embrace when he spread his arms for me. "Look after my girl," I whispered in his ear.

"I'll love her with everything that's in me. I swear." Stepping back, he squeezed my arm and winked. "You can do this. You're a big tough chick."

"Take lots of photos." Fliss pulled me into a hug. "Stay in touch. I want updates on every step of your journey. Even the boring stuff."

I nodded, resting my chin on her shoulder and squeezing tight.

"Love you, Flissy."

"Love you, Chuck. Come home soon."

I pulled back, put on the bravest smile I could muster then spun and walked inside.

Finding the right counter was easy. Walking to it was another story…until I got a text from Nixon.

Travel challenge—Day 1: Take a photo of the craziest-looking person on the plane.

I'll expect a snap as soon as you touch down in Hawaii.

Be safe, gorgeous. I'll be thinking of you the whole

time.

Love you xx

Below that was a series of emojis that made me laugh, and then he pasted a link to "Leaving on a Jet Plane" by Me First and Gimme Gimmes.

I scrambled for my earplugs and soon had the song blasting in my ears. It made me grin, and then it made me laugh...and then it made me dance to the counter to check in with an excitement that only a traveler could feel.

I was on my way.

And Nixon was coming with me.

THIRTY-EIGHT

NIXON

I missed her. It'd been two days since she left and I was pining like a freaking teenage girl with an uber crush.

Staring at my phone, I smiled at the most recent photo Charlie had sent me. It was a breathtaking sunset that she'd just watched from the beach.

Damn, I wanted to be there, see it with my own eyes.

Glancing at my desk, I spotted the acceptance letter from Columbia. Gently sliding it out from beneath my pile of old textbooks, I slowly read it again.

My parents were so freaking proud the day it arrived.

Wrinkling my nose, I scrunched it into a tight wad and threw it towards the trash can.

It hit the rim and landed on the floor…right next to my father's shiny black shoe.

He glanced down at the paper and then across the room at me.

"Can I come in?"

I just stared at him, not sure what to say.

I was still pretty pissed about what he'd done, and I'd told him so. Ripped shreds off him the second I'd gotten home from saying goodbye to Charlie. It'd been a shock, considering it was three o'clock in the morning. A hell of a way to wake up.

We hadn't really spoken again since.

I would have moved out already, but I had no place to go and I wasn't ready to set up in New York yet. I didn't even know if I wanted to go.

But what would that mean if I didn't?

I wasn't naive enough to deny I'd had a privileged life. Up to that point, my parents had basically covered all my expenses. My constantly topped-up trust fund meant I'd never had to want for anything…other than Charlie.

It made me dumb and immature to think I hadn't even considered this before. But if I followed my heart, I had to face the reality that I could very soon be homeless and broke.

I glanced at my father, who was still loitering outside my door.

With a heavy sigh, I tipped my head and silently

told him to come in.

He shuffled into my room, perching on the edge of my bed and gazing at the wall of academic trophies and certificates.

He didn't say anything, just stared up at that damn wall.

My radio was playing softly in the background but my ears picked up on a familiar tune and I grimaced, realizing the song was nailing it.

"Rather Be."

Hell yeah, I'd rather be anywhere than where I was.

Sitting in my beige room that Mom had designed, painfully watching my father in his black slacks and white shirt struggle to form a sentence…not exactly a breathtaking sunset in Hawaii with the woman I loved.

"If you gave me a chance…" The singer shot an arrow into my heart as she kept singing, reminding me that the only place on Earth I really wanted to be was by Charlie's side.

Broke or not, I wanted to be with my girl.

Turning towards my stereo, I gazed at the display panel and was struck yet again by how much music had been trying to speak to me since that snowbound moment in New York. All the songs on the road trip, my "Crashed the Wedding" moment—it kept leading me to Charlie.

Closing my eyes, it hit me with the force of a wrecking ball.

I was a stupid idiot.

Had I been deaf the whole time?

The music had finally convinced me to be with Charlie and what was I doing? Sitting at home with my parents, *not* being with Charlie.

"I don't want to go to Columbia," I blurted, surprised by how damn good those words felt coming out of my mouth.

Dad's expression bunched with pain and then he slowly nodded like he somehow knew this was coming. "What do you want to do, then?"

"I want to be with Charlie," I croaked. "That's all I've ever wanted."

Squeezing his eyes shut, he pinched the bridge of his nose.

"And it's not just some young, blind love talking here. We had dreams, plans. Things we *both* wanted to do. And now she's off doing them and I'm stuck here, missing her. Missing out on the life I wanted. All because you put your nose in and screwed everything up!"

Gritting his teeth, Dad shot me a hard look. "I was trying to protect you."

"Yet you destroyed the one thing that was most precious to me."

He scrubbed a hand down his face and he held his mouth, obviously fighting strong emotions.

With a soft sigh, I looked to the floor and murmured, "I know you were only trying to do what you thought was right. But you were wrong. You were so wrong."

"We were terrified of losing you." His brown eyes were pleading with me to understand. "You didn't see your mother. How afraid she was. She had visions of you leaving and never coming back. I couldn't handle watching her return to that place of…darkness. The hours she cried over Reagan. All that emotion, I just… I couldn't watch her go through it again."

"I wasn't dying. I was leaving the country for a while. We had every intention of coming back."

"You're our only son," he croaked. "We needed to keep this family together."

"You could have, so easily. If you'd just let Charlie in."

He swallowed. "It would have been so hard on you both. High school was fine. You hung out together there, but life…actual life? She doesn't fit. That may sound snobby, but it's true. All of our friends…They would have mocked her. It'd be like trying to enter a unicorn into a pedigree dog show. She's so…out there, Nixon." He pointed at my computer screen behind me. "I mean, her hair is blue. It's blue!"

I glanced over my shoulder and grinned at my screensaver. It was the selfie Charlie took for the Day 2 challenge I sent her. She had to take a pic wearing something that made her laugh. She had a big pair of heart-shaped shades on and was pulling the cutest face.

Brushing my fingers over the screen, I turned back to my father and looked him in the eye.

"Will you cut me off financially if I don't go to New York?" My voice was hard, my gaze hopefully telling him that I knew exactly what he'd said to her.

His eyebrows dipped together, guilt and disappointment running over his expression. A heavy sigh made his entire body slump. "Truth is, I wouldn't have done any of the things I threatened Charlie with. I was just trying to scare her."

"You asshole," I murmured.

Again, his expression was pained and desperate for me to understand.

All I could do was glare at him.

"We're going to lose you if we don't support your choices, aren't we?"

"Yes." There was no point bullshitting. I wasn't losing Charlie again, and if they were going to make me choose, then that was their problem.

It kind of hurt to say it. After everything we'd been through, all the energy I'd poured into making them proud, it hurt like nothing else to know what they'd done. But I wasn't immune to the pain they'd experienced losing Reagan either.

I wanted to be the good son, but they were forcing me into rebellion.

"It's my life, Dad. I was old enough back then to make my own decisions, and I'm sure as hell old enough now. I'm not wasting any more time living the life *you* think is best for me. I don't want to be a lawyer. I should never have given up on journalism." I shook my head. "It's time to follow my heart, or I'm going to die a miserable loser."

"She's coming back for you," he whispered hopefully.

"When? If you think I'm just going to sit back and take this for one more day, then think again.

Even if you cut me off, I *will* find a way to make this happen. I'm sick of waiting for my heart to be in the same place I am. I can't do it anymore."

"And you won't have to," Mom said from the doorway. Tears were streaming down her cheeks. Wiping them away with her delicate fingers, she caught Dad's eye and put on a brave smile. "I understand what you were trying to do by scaring Charlie away." With a little sniff, she stepped into the room and reached out for Dad's hand. He took it and gently brushed his lips over her knuckles. "I love that you were trying to protect me, but don't you remember Nixon's heartache? I guess part of me was relieved that she'd gone, because she did scare me. I thought she was going to steal my son and lead him astray, but... I was also so mad with her for making Nixon suffer that way. It hurt to watch him so heartbroken. And I don't want him to go through that again."

Dad's face bunched in agony while Mom cast her eyes to me.

"I want you to be happy. And you seem pretty convinced that traveling with her will make you that way. I have to trust you now. You're an amazing man, and I love you. So that trust fund is yours, Nixon. You use it for whatever you need to."

"As long as you use it wisely," Dad grumbled.

I sniggered at him. "You know, with the amount you spout about my intelligence, you act like I have none."

Closing his eyes with a sigh, he smoothed back his hair.

"It's called trust, Dad. Mom's willing to give it a try. Maybe you should too."

Mom let out a watery laugh, then sniffed when I looked at her. Her lips wobbled and a fresh set of tears filled her eyes. Rising from my chair, I walked across the room and wrapped my arms around her.

"Letting go means you *won't* lose me. You're doing the right thing, Mom. I love you, and I promise I'll stay in touch."

Stay in touch.

The thought made my insides zing.

I was doing it.

I was finally doing something for me. Something I wanted.

It was an amazing feeling, and as I hugged my mom tight, I couldn't help the excited grin stretching across my face.

THIRTY-NINE

CHARLIE

My week in Hawaii was over. It had been a fantastic time. I made friends with a few people in the hostel and we hung out a little. They were nothing close to Nixon though. All the things I'd done without him—surfing lessons, scuba diving, visiting Pearl Harbor—he would have loved all of it. It made me sad that I could only show him photos and videos. Sure, we laughed about it on Skype, but it wasn't the same.

I missed my man.

As I stepped into the airport, I checked the board and noticed flights for LAX. It was tempting to go back home, but I'd already paid for my next flight. I couldn't turn back after such a short time.

Dumping my pack on the ground, I pulled out my phone, hoping for a little inspiration. Nixon had been with me daily, keeping me on track and living my dream.

I wanted him beside me, but I knew I couldn't type that. He had plans and parents to deal with. New York was waiting.

With a sniff, I reread his last text, then grinned when my phone dinged with a new one. Opening it up, I read the words and frowned.

Travel challenge—Day 7: Find the best-looking guy in the airport and ask him to travel the next leg with you. Trust me, it'll be a fun adventure.

Love you always xx

With a snort, I shook my head and read the message again.

He wanted me to what?

That couldn't be right. I wasn't going off with some good-looking guy.

"You are batshit crazy, Holloway," I mumbled, trying to figure out the perfect comeback.

Looking up, I scanned my surroundings for inspiration and then froze.

I found him—the good-looking guy I was supposed to travel with.

A burst of laughter shot out of me so fast and loud I scared the man walking past me.

He gave me an odd look and hurried by, but I

couldn't even apologize.

All I could do was stand in shock as my dreams fell perfectly into place.

Nixon stood across from me, a dopey smile on his face. He was in jean shorts and a black T-shirt, looking like the ultimate tourist with the overstuffed pack at his feet. His hair was product-free and flopped across his forehead.

He'd never looked sexier.

And I didn't think twice.

Leaving my pack against the wall, I ran across the space and straight into his arms. He caught me with a laugh while I let out an excited scream and wrapped my legs around his waist. My flip-flops fell off but I didn't even care. Nixon held me tight and met my hungry lips with a grin.

Cupping my ass, he kissed me solidly while I wrapped my arms around his neck.

In need of air, I pulled back and squeezed his shoulders. "What are you doing here?"

"I'm looking for a travel buddy." He winked and I kissed him again.

"I can't believe it." I finally breathed, running my fingers into his hair and wanting to get lost in those brown eyes of his. "How? When did you…? I…"

He laughed at my speechlessness, placing me back on the floor and grabbing his pack so we could walk back to mine. I shoved my flip-flops back on and took his hand while we walked to my pack.

"Thing is, Charlie Watson, I'm miserable

without you. What's the point of going to New York when I feel that way? I never really wanted to be a lawyer."

My eyes bulged. "What did your parents say?"

"Well, they haven't cut me off." He shrugged.

"Bet they're still not happy about it."

"Does it even matter?" He cupped my face, his fingers curling into my blue hair. "All I want is to be with you. To see the world, with you. All this time, you didn't think you could fit into my world. And maybe you can't. But I can fit into yours." His eyes burned with conviction. "We're good for each other. You bring out the best in me. I want you. I need you." The edge of his mouth lifted with a smile. "You think you're a flight risk, but I know how to handle that now."

My forehead wrinkled.

His smile grew. "I'll just chase you. I should have chased you four years ago. I'm not making that mistake again. You fly, I fly." He kissed the tip of my nose. "No matter who you're with or what you're doing, there's no other place on Earth I'd rather be than right beside you."

I'd never loved him more.

Tears glassed my eyes while he was talking. I gave in to them, letting them trickle down my cheeks as I let out a giddy laugh. Wrapping my arms around him, I rose to my tiptoes and hugged him tight. It was such a relief to know I wouldn't have to let go for a long time to come. Cupping the back of my head, he held me against him and I closed my eyes, this warm kind of joy buzzing through my entire body.

"So..." Nixon brushed his nose across my cheek. "Where are you taking me?"

I giggled and pulled back to look at him. "New Zealand."

"Nice." His eyebrows rose. "I've always wanted to go there."

I giggled again. Geez, I sounded like a fourteen-year-old girl, but I couldn't help it. I was standing in Nixon's arms and those plans...those dreams that we came up with in Yosemite were finally coming true.

"Well, as much as I want to stand here kissing you all day, why don't we go see if we can squeeze me onto a flight?"

"I can rebook mine."

"Or I can meet you in New Zealand."

"Forget it." I frowned. "I'd rather sleep on a dirty airport floor for the next three days than have to leave you again. I am so over that!"

Nixon grinned and brushed his lips across mine. "You'll never have to do it again. No more goodbyes for us."

"Promise?"

"Promise."

And he sealed it with a kiss.

EPILOGUE

NIXON

"Okay, what are we telling them this time?" I turned to Charlie and grinned, loving the excited look she got whenever we were getting ready to record another YouTube clip.

We'd started a channel in New Zealand, posting daily updates on our trip. The clips were never more than a couple of minutes, but we'd try to choose one awesome thing from each day to share with our friends and family at home.

At first, it'd just been for them, but the Chix Travel Diary had grown in popularity and we now had thousands of subscribers who checked in for each episode.

"Let's get the mountains in the background and tell them about the temple."

I nodded and got ready to set up for recording.

We only had a few days left in Nepal before flying to New Delhi.

The last four months had gone by in what seemed like a rush. New Zealand, Australia, Bali, Philippines, Vietnam, Thailand, Laos. We'd met the most amazing people, seen the most amazing sights, and there was still more to come.

In an effort not to run out of money, we'd brainstormed ways to earn as we traveled. My trust fund and Charlie's savings would only keep us going for so long, and I kind of wanted the liberty of spending cash *I'd* earned rather than continuing to use my parents' money. If anything, I wanted to keep that money for necessities only...plus a few donations we'd made along the way. Some of the poverty we'd seen was a real eye-opener, and it was impossible not to give some to charity. It was the least we could do.

So as a way to earn some cash-on-the-go, Charlie had started selling her photography and was making a mint on each picture. However, the sales were sometimes sporadic, so I'd spent a few weeks contacting every travel magazine I could and had managed to score myself a weekly column for an online one, plus a monthly column for a glossy one in LA. Dad helped me hook it up. It'd been a beautiful moment.

Charlie and I were also working on publishing a

series of travel books as we went. One per country, filled with photos, guides, travel tips—anything useful to travelers on a tight budget looking to do something similar. Readers were starting to take note and between the different income sources, we were getting enough to fund our flights.

The thought of returning home seemed so farfetched it was almost laughable.

Our plans took us through the next twelve months at least, and we wanted to keep going for as long as we could.

The lifestyle suited us.

We'd slept in hostels, tents, a few nights of luxury in the odd hotel, but mostly we were "roughing it."

And I was the happiest I'd ever been.

Waking up beside Charlie on a daily basis suited me. Experiencing life together, the good and the bad, the stressful and the peaceful. We somehow worked our way through it all and continued to come out stronger.

"Okay." Charlie stood behind me, wrapping her arms around my waist and resting her chin on my shoulder.

She must have been on the very tips of her toes, but the shot on screen was perfect.

I pressed Record and we grinned at the camera before doing a slow circle as we captured the Himalayas behind us.

"Hey, everyone." Charlie's voice was bright and vibrant, just like her hair. The ends were still blue, but she'd added a layer of purple, which looked amazing. "So we're in Kathmandu. Today we checked out Bodhnath Temple, which was so incredibly like wow."

"Totally wow." I nodded.

"So, I'll post some of my pics online…along with a certain video."

Charlie's dry voice and expression made me laugh.

"Yes, thank you to Everett Marshall for today's challenge." I grimaced and poked my tongue out before grinning at the camera.

Charlie laughed in my ear. "Yeah, so it turns out Swan Puka is actually goat lungs," she explained to the camera. "We ate goat lungs today, people. Thanks for that, Everett."

We'd no doubt get a lot of comments on that one, plus some more challenges. The idea had taken off pretty soon into our trip. It'd been fueled by Chaos, who got the whole thing going after Fliss found out how I'd started Charlie's trip for her.

Some of the challenges were pretty insane, but so far we'd managed to pull all of them off, including sex in the ocean (Flick's idea—we didn't video that one) and breaking into a spontaneous rendition of "Geronimo" at some random restaurant in Thailand. That one had been from Jane and Harry, and in typical Charlie style, she managed to get the whole place singing. That was one of our most liked Daily Challenge videos.

Surprisingly enough, my parents commented on almost every clip we posted. It meant a lot and was a way to help mend some bridges.

Charlie spoke a little more about our day in Kathmandu, including some history about the temple before we signed off with a local greeting. We were trying to at least learn "hello," "goodbye" and "thank you" in the language of every country we visited. It was working pretty well so far, and people appreciated the effort.

Tucking the camera into my day pack, I hitched it onto my shoulder and then smiled down at my girl. Wrapping my arm around her waist, I pulled her against me and wiggled my eyebrows.

She grinned. "What's that look for?"

"Well, we've kind of seen everything we wanted to today, so I'm having visions of you, me, a little hotel room about five minutes down the road, and a whole lot of afternoon delight."

Biting back her grin, Charlie shook her head. "You're never going to get enough of me, are you?"

"Nope, never." I winked at her, loving the smile on her face.

"Well then, Mr. Nix, you better just take me to bed and show me exactly what afternoon delight means."

With a soft chuckle, I took her hand and started walking for our little hotel, humming "Afternoon Delight" as I went. She snorted and slapped my arm, taking charge in the music department and changing the song to "Can't Get Enough of You Baby" by Smash Mouth. She changed the word "I" to "you" and belted out, "You can't get enough of me, baby" at the top of her lungs. I wasn't about to let her win, so we ended up doing a song battle all the way back to the hotel—laughing, singing, and basically being Chix.

The way we were always meant to be.

Two best friends.

A whole wide world.

And enough love to last a lifetime.

THE END

Thank you so much for reading *Rather Be*. If you've enjoyed it and would like to show me some support, please consider leaving an honest review.

KEEP READING TO FIND OUT ABOUT THE FINAL CHAOS NOVELLA...

The final Chaos novella belongs to:

Jace & Jenna

SONGBIRD

Due for release in August 2017

Some risks are worth taking…

Being the drummer for a world-famous rock band is the job Jace always dreamed of…but it comes at a price. Constant press, misleading articles, and a slew of fans who can't always be trusted have made him question whether the lifestyle he's chosen is worth the risk.

But he loves drumming, and he doesn't want to quit on his rock band family, Chaos…until he hears the voice of Jenna, a mysterious woman who captures his heart at first song.

Jenna knows all about risks, and falling for a famous rock star is the last thing she needs. She has far more important things to do…like staying hidden and keeping her secrets safe. But Jace is so sweet and different—he makes it impossible to resist him. Jenna knows she's playing with fire by dating a guy who's instantly recognized wherever he goes…whose face is splashed across magazine covers and television gossip shows.

For Jace, Jenna just might be a risk worth taking. But Jenna knows that some risks are too big, too great. Especially when her life is on the line.

This novella is an exclusive story for newsletter subscribers only. If you'd like to receive the story in August 2017, then please sign up to become a Songbird Novels Reader. You'll also receive free copies of the first two Chaos novellas—Angel Eyes and Complicated—when you sign up..

http://www.subscribepage.com/songbird-readers

You can find the other Songbird Novels on Amazon.

FEVER
Ella & Cole's story

BULLETPROOF
Morgan & Sean's story

EVERYTHING
Jody & Leo's story

HOME
Rachel & Josh's story

TRUE LOVE
Nessa & Jimmy's story

TROUBLEMAKER
Marcus & Kelly's story

ROUGH WATER
Justin & Sarah's story

GERONIMO
Harry & Jane's story

HOLE HEARTED
Troy & Cassie's story

NOTE FROM THE AUTHOR

The last Songbird Novel. I can't believe it! I've tried to make this book as special as I can for you. I wanted to gift you little cameos from each of the books—stories I have adored working on.

Thank you so much for being a part of this journey with me. I published Fever nearly three years ago. It feels like a lifetime. So much has happened in this Songbird world since then. Each and every novel holds a very special place in my heart, and it's a true privilege to finish the collection with Nixon and Charlie.

These two characters were with me right from the beginning. When I first mapped out the books, I knew I wanted to finish with them. They were actually the couple that inspired me to connect all the dots and have characters from previous books feature in all the other stories. It's been such a treat.

I will miss this world, but after Jace's novella, I'm ready to move on to something new.

The thing I'll miss the most, other than these wonderful characters who feel like real people to me, is the music. I often go back and listen to the playlists I created for each book. It brings back memories, but it's also a chance to enjoy some really fantastic songs.

I know I've said thank you a few times, but seriously - THANK YOU for reading this book. I hope it's warmed your heart and inspired you in some way.

May music connect you with the ones you love, make the memories last forever, and help you through the emotional times when the only thing you can do is listen and cry.

May you dance.

May you sing.

May you love.

xx
Melissa

Keep reading for the playlist and the link to find it on Spotify.

RATHER BE SOUNDTRACK

(Please note: The songs listed below are not always the original versions, but the ones I chose to listen to while constructing this book. The songs are listed in the order they appear.)

DON'T WORRY BE HAPPY
Performed by Bobby McFerrin

HAVE FUN GO MAD
Performed by Blair

THUNDERBIRDS ARE GO
Performed by Busted

IN TOO DEEP
Performed by Sum 41

BREAK ME DOWN
Performed by Tenth Avenue North

RAISE YOUR GLASS
Performed by P!nk

DREAMING ALONE
Performed by Against The Current

SHE MOVES IN HER OWN WAY
Performed by The Kooks

WHY DON'T YOU LOVE ME
Performed by Hot Chelle Rae & Demi Lovato

CLOSER
Performed by The Chainsmokers & Halsey

LONG WAY HOME
Performed by 5 Seconds of Summer

THIS TOWN
Performed by Niall Horan

WE ARE YOUNG
Performed by Glee Cast

GOOD TIME
Performed by Owl City & Carly Rae Jepsen

JUST A DREAM
Performed by Jason Chen & Joseph Vincent

LIVE LIFE LOUD
Performed by Hawk Nelson

ANOTHER YOU (ANOTHER WAY)
Performed by Against the Current

EVERYTHING I DIDN'T SAY
Performed by 5 Seconds of Summer

WE BELONG
Performed by Sheppard

LET ME DOWN EASY
Performed by Sheppard

EMPTY
Performed by The Click Five

11 BLOCKS
Performed by Wrabel

GRAVITY
Performed by Against the Current

CARRY ON
Performed by Fun

CUPS
Performed by The Barden Bellas

NEVER SURRENDER
Performed by Skillet

COMEBACK KID
Performed by Against the Current

CRASHED THE WEDDING
Performed by Busted

SAY YOU WON'T LET GO
Performed by James Arthur

HAPPY TOGETHER
Performed by Simple Plan

LEAVING ON A JET PLANE
Performed by Me First and the Gimme Gimmes

RATHER BE
Performed by Clean Bandit & Jess Glynne

AFTERNOON DELIGHT
Performed by Glee Cast

CAN'T GET ENOUGH OF YOU BABY
Performed by Smash Mouth

To enhance your reading experience, you can listen along to the playlist for **https://open.spotify.com/user/12146962946/playlist/2WCQHbpoadAufvL1pOcssu**

ACKNOWLEDGEMENTS

Thank you so much to everyone who had input in producing *Rather Be.*
It ended up being a tough story to complete, and I'm so grateful to the people who helped me.

My critique readers: Cassie, Beth, Renee, Lenore and Rae. Your insights were so helpful. Thank you for always giving me so much time and making me think about how I can make the story the best it can be. I loved our little impromptu discussions. It felt like we were all writing the book together :)

My editor: Beth. Thanks for stepping up last minute and being so wonderful to work with.

My proofreaders: I love you guys. Thank you for your time and attention.

My advanced reading team: You guys are awesome!

My cover designer and photographer: Regina. I love this cover so much. You nailed it, clever lady.

Songbirds & Playmakers: My daily interactions with you guys are so much fun and you make this job so amazing. Thanks for your constant support and encouragement.

My family: Thanks for letting me harp on about writing. Thanks for the pep talks. Thanks for the hugs, and loving me without fail.

My Lord Jesus: My inspiration, the music in my heart. Thank you for your daily friendship and abounding love. You make all things possible.

OTHER BOOKS BY MELISSA PEARL

The Songbird Novels

Fever—Bulletproof—Everything—Home—True Love—Troublemaker—Rough Water—Geronimo Hole Hearted—Rather Be

The Space Between Heartbeats

Plus two novellas:
The Space Before & The Space Beyond

The Fugitive Series

I Know Lucy — Set Me Free

The Masks Series

True Colors — Two-Faced
Snake Eyes — Poker Face

The Time Spirit Trilogy

Golden Blood — Black Blood — Pure Blood

The Elements Trilogy

Unknown — Unseen — Unleashed

The Mica & Lexy Series

Forbidden Territory—Forbidden Waters

Find out more on Melissa Pearl's website:
www.melissapearlauthor.com

ABOUT MELISSA PEARL

Melissa Pearl is a kiwi girl living in Hamilton, New Zealand. She trained as an elementary school teacher but has always had a passion for writing and finally completed her first manuscript in 2003. She has been writing ever since, and the more she learns, the more she loves it.

She writes young adult and new adult fiction in a variety of romance genres—paranormal, fantasy, suspense, and contemporary. Her goal as a writer is to give readers the pleasure of escaping their everyday lives for a while and losing themselves in a journey…one that will make them laugh, cry, and swoon.

MELISSA PEARL ONLINE

Website:
www.melissapearlauthor.com

YouTube Channel:
www.youtube.com/user/melissapearlauthor

Facebook:
www.facebook.com/melissapearlauthor

Instagram:
instagram.com/melissapearlauthor

Twitter:
twitter.com/MelissaPearlG

Pinterest:
www.pinterest.com/melissapearlg

CPSIA information can be obtained
at www.ICGtesting.com
Printed in the USA
LVOW12s0938020318
568460LV00001B/132/P